I0626158

A Demon
in the Desert

Grimluk, Demon Hunter – Vol 1

Ashe Armstrong

Copyright © 2015 Ashe Armstrong

Cover Art by Bob Kehl
Cover & Interior Design by Ashe Armstrong

All rights reserved. This book or any portion thereof may
not be reproduced or used in any manner whatsoever
without the express written permission of the publisher
except for the use of brief quotations in a book review.

This book is a work of fiction. Names, characters, events,
and locations are fictitious or are used fictitiously. Any
resemblances to actual events or persons, living or dead,
are entirely coincidental.

First Edition, June 2015

ISBN: 0996340904
ISBN-13: 978-0-9963409-0-8

DEDICATION

To my star- I couldn't have done this without you.

CONTENTS

ACKNOWLEDGMENTS

Thank you to the friends who encouraged me at the start and kept encouraging me as I went along.

Special thanks to those who offered notes.

And gratitude to my Kickstarter backers, new acquaintances and old friends alike. At the very least, you showed me I could find an audience.

Chapter 1

The summer sun hung high in the air, casting blinding light and heavy heat in equal measures. Even under the shade of the slender trees that covered the worn road, the heat was inescapable. Light poured down through the wide-spread canopies of brilliant blue-green leaves, occasionally looking like stained glass to those who happened to look up. The treetops combined with a dull, flickering breeze to tease relief. The heat was oppressive.

The road was long, mostly dirt and weeds with ruts from countless wagons and buggies surrounded by a carpet of thick, green grass that looked to be yellowing somewhat in the heat. A lone figure cloaked in a long, black coat, the tails covered in the patina of a nomad wandered down the road. A wide-brimmed hat, wrapped by a leather band holding thirteen canine teeth, kept the sunlight at bay. An elk-skin bag hung at his side, with several bulging waterskins tied to it.

The figure walked at a steady pace, down the center of the road, between the wagon ruts before being stopped by a disparate group of people, led by a human woman with a shaved head. Behind her trailed a pair of tan dwarves, fraternal twins, with long, red hair and beards, followed by a tall, elf man with dirty-blond hair, and a dark-skinned halfling woman with a mop of tight, black curls. Their leader scratched her fuzzy head. The whole group wore torn jeans, heavy boots, and stained work shirts. The woman wore a blue jacket as well.

"Greetings, traveler," she said, bowing, arms spread wide. "My name is Lilanda. These are my associates, and we'd like to politely inform you that we're robbing you. We're generous though so we'll let you keep your clothes and boots as long as you acquiesce quickly and quietly." Lilanda pulled out an old revolver and motioned with it. "Hurry now, orc, we prefer to avoid bloodshed when possible."

The orc was an imposing figure, standing taller even than the elf. Eyes the color of charcoal looked up, staring hard into Lilanda's gray eyes, his jaw set tight. He took a step forward. The bandit leader held up her gun, pulling the hammer back, locked in the orc's gaze.

"I see, ya gotta do things the hard way. Fine, fine, don't say we didn't try," she said, punctuating the statement with an exasperated sigh. "Dreya, Druen, convince him."

The dwarf twins each pulled out long, thick knives that looked more like short swords. The halfling grinned, picking her nails idly with a stiletto dagger. The orc pulled his coat back as the twins moved towards him revealing a gun belt hanging not quite loosely on black-denim clad hips. The belt was plain, browned leather, only adorned with brass cartridges slotted into loops. A matching holster lay against his right hip housing a massive revolver with a grip of reddish sandalwood. The dwarves froze.

"Since you've been so polite, I'll offer my own politeness in return," the orc said. "Name's Grimluk and if you'd like to continue having use of your limbs, I'd advise you to back off." His hand hovered over the butt of his gun.

Dreya and Druen looked back at Lilanda, unsure of what to do. "They don't usually fight back," Dreya observed, her brother nodding in agreement.

"Don't fucking stand there with your thumbs up your asses, get his shit!" she commanded.

The twins looked back at Grimluk, who shook his head. "I'm gonna gut ya and wear your tusks as trophies!" Druen shouted before he charged, thrusting his big knife at the orc's stomach. Grimluk swatted Druen's arm away and then kicked him in the chest so hard it threw the dwarf into his sister.

Before Lilanda had time to register what had just happened, Grimluk had drawn his gun and fired on her. Her own pistol exploded, almost ripping her trigger finger off and breaking several others. The elf and halfling took off running back into the woods.

"I'd tend to your friend here. That hand's gonna take some time to heal," Grimluk said to the pile of dwarves.

"Who the fuck *are* you?" Lilanda asked with a shudder.

"No one of consequence," Grimluk replied with a grin, resuming his journey.

The road ended at the town of Border Rest, one of the few outpost towns to crop up on the borders of the Wastelands over the past fifty years. As Grimluk got closer, the trees and grass started to grow more sparse and patchy. The grass began to look like a ruined carpet, scratched and weathered, all but dead. The trees that remained, slender to begin with, were almost skeletal now, with few leaves and a dry bark, further baked by the harsh sun. Border Rest itself was an ugly little patch of dust and grime. Several of the buildings looked like they'd crumble in a stiff breeze and seemed to voice a near constant protest with groans and creaks.

Most of the locals were ugly too. Various traders, merchants, and vagabonds, as well as the asshole that owned the only saloon and inn, the Dancing Dwarf. An old human, notorious for serving watered down booze and food that may have been actual cooked shit. Rumors in the surrounding towns suggested that some of the merchants made deals with local bandits like the gang Grimluk had encountered. There were no shortage of travelers who had been mugged on the road only to find their belongings being sold in town. No one was ever surprised though since there were no peacekeepers in Border Rest. The only reason anyone built anything on the borderlands was for money. If you were traveling into the Wastelands, even as a well-armed trading caravan, you needed to be stocked and prepared or the Wastes would swallow you up and, occasionally, not even spit up your bones.

One of the few constants here, and anywhere else, however were the bounty boards. The few towns and settlements that survived the genesis of the Wastelands and carried on sometimes required outside help. Whether a call for a supply caravan, new laborers, or a cry for a hunter of some kind, all the border towns were connected through an arcane communication system that let anyone interested check for work or trade. Most folks called it the "magi-tell."

Grimluk was headed for one such board. He was a demon hunter, just off a small job at a farm a few miles back and ready for new work. Evil never slept, as the humans were fond of saying.

As he came into the town, a sunburned elf with bloodshot, emerald green eyes and a crooked nose tried to sell him magical beans. They were, in fact, black beans that had long since lost any use or flavor. Grimluk passed him by without a word. The elf, who took offense to this, hurled obscenities and then the beans at him.

He made his way through a busy street full of travelers. The street dumped into a four-way intersection. To his left, stalls sat open with humans and elves hocking their wares. These stalls sat across from the general store and the blacksmith on his right. Further down sat the livery and the Dancing Dwarf.

Grimluk saw the crystal antenna for the magi-tell standing tall on a building behind the stalls, facing the other road. He started to make his way towards the building but was interrupted by a particularly loud, middle-aged human man, who was quite certain he'd found a new customer. The man's sweaty, balding head glinted in the sun as he began his spiel.

"My friend, you look like a man in need of a good blade. Especially out here, in the *Wastelands*," he said, flourishing "Wastelands." "There are strange beasts around every corner. But have no fear, you're in luck! My blades are absolutely guaranteed to ward off and wound any creatures of darkness that may beset you! Guaranteed, friend!"

Grimluk groaned and tried to step around him.

The blade-seller persisted.

"Ah, ol' Sal sees that worry in your eyes. You think you can't afford such a wondrous product, my friend, but because I value the safety of all who venture these parts, I can assure you that my prices are more than reasonable."

"Move," Grimluk rumbled.

"Trust me, friend, you've never seen blades like this before," Sal bellowed, producing a large, blue knife for him. "These knives were crafted by an elvish sorcerer to fight demons, my friend. Demons!"

Grimluk looked into the older man's pale blue eyes and took the knife in his right hand. Sal smiled and stroked his gray beard. He reached into his coat, behind his back and unsheathed his own blade. Though similarly shaped, Grimluk's knife was slightly bigger and appeared to be forged of several materials that shimmered in the sunlight like a dark rainbow. Near the guard, the blade was etched with a symbol that resembled a stick with five branches. Grimluk held his own knife flat out, so the blade was horizontal.

"I have a blade," he told Sal as he brought the tip of the blue knife to lay against his own. He pushed the blue blade into his own. It resisted for a second, then the tip began to crack as the blue blade splintered, chunks of brittle metal falling to their feet.

Sal's face was a mask of shock. "Hey, buddy! You broke it you-"

"If you're gonna keep sellin' these pieces of shit as demon-killers, you should probably know when you're talking to an actual demon hunter." The blue blade, and Sal's face, dropped as Grimluk moved on.

Behind him, he could hear people snickering at Sal.

The porch of the bounty office held a slew of people looking for work. A pair of orcs, mismatched in size and dressed garishly, chatted excitedly with each other. The smaller one made mention of treasure. A lone elf under a black hat and coat stood against the walls just outside the door. A curved sword hung at his back while a bandoleer of white oak stakes hung across his chest. Further down the boardwalk stood a motley group of an elf, a man, and a dwarf. All three looked haggard, like they'd been traveling non-stop for years at a breakneck pace. Grimluk figured they were probably caravan guards waiting for a new job.

Grimluk passed through the open door of the bounty office. Inside sat a few more people waiting for work. Off to his right was a desk where a halfling sat with a huge, black ledger. The halfling had dark skin and eyes and a head of squared, rough hair. On his nose sat a pair of spectacles. He looked bored but nonetheless very professional.

In the back of the small building was the bounty board. The thing covered the entirety of the back wall, split into four sections; Hunting, Guarding, Labor, and Other. Each section was currently empty, which explained the others waiting around. Grimluk stood silently, staring at the empty board and grunted. He would have to wait as well. He stepped back outside, safe from the beating sun under the porch, and turned to the vampire hunter.

"How long have you been waiting?" Grimluk inquired.

The elf looked up with eyes the color of autumn leaves. "Days," he said curtly.

Grimluk nodded. He looked out at the squat little town, a sudden gust of wind blowing dirt down the street he'd come from. *Might as well get a room and some food*, he thought, heading for the Dancing Dwarf. The place smelled like stale beer. A tan elf sat at a piano to the left of the door, playing some sort of silly tune that several drunken patrons were singing along with from behind him. Grimluk couldn't tell for sure but it sounded like they were singing "low-ee, low-ee."

Grimluk walked to the bar and ordered a plate of ham, beans, and a couple of biscuits along with the house beer. It tasted just like the room smelled. So did the food. He requested a room, pleased to find that the Dancing Dwarf had a few rooms to accommodate the orcs that passed through. After checking out his room, he decided to pass some time back downstairs playing some penny poker.

A few hours later, Grimluk had managed to come away a little bit richer. After scooping up the pile of bronze pennies and silver bilts, he made his way back over to the bounty board, hoping maybe a new job had posted while he was busy. The travelers he'd seen earlier had dispersed, the boardwalk empty now. Grimluk moved to the side as a pale-green half-orc with a long, black ponytail made his way through the doorway.

"Pardon, friend," he said, nodding at the younger man, who returned the gesture as he headed in the direction Grimluk had come. Grimluk noticed the shield-badge marked "Captain" on the man's black, leather vest, as well as the gun and saber that hung on each hip. Grimluk thought maybe the town was finally making an effort to bring some peacekeepers in to protect travelers.

The evening sun still shone bright enough that the halfling behind the desk hadn't had to light any lanterns yet. Grimluk spotted the ragged piece of parchment pinned to the board, alone and yellowed under the Hunting section. He stepped forward to inspect it, moving his jaw idly, his tusks bouncing with the movement. Grimluk smiled. Luck was with him it seemed.

There, in big letters at the top, were the words "**DEMON HUNTER NEEDED**." He read on.

Mining town in need of help
Bounty is 5 gluts
See Captain Trilgor at the
Dancing Dwarf, Border Rest

Grimluk nodded before returning to the Dwarf. The barman pointed him towards a table in the back, currently occupied by the half-orc and a couple of tankards of the house piss water. The poor man nearly choked on his first swallow, holding the tankard out with a look of contempt. He looked up as Grimluk approached.

"Can you believe this shit?" he asked, holding out the tankard.

Grimluk laughed. "I've had better backwash." The young Captain laughed. "You Trilgor?"

"Reckon so, last I checked."

"I understand you got a demon that needs

killin'."

"I do," Trilgor said, taking another drink of his beer. "You a hunter?"

"A demon hunter to boot."

Trilgor pushed a chair out with his boot. "Have a seat."

"So let's hear about this demon of yours," Grimluk said as he dropped lightly into the chair.

Trilgor shook his head at the tankard. "You think if I threatened to beat the brewer with this that he'd learn how to make a decent ale?"

Grimluk grinned. "Probably not. That'd require he give a shit first. S'pose it couldn't hurt to try though."

Trilgor sighed and set the tankard back down before leaning forward, half-resting on the table. "Right, so, the demon. Thing's seem pretty bad. Been about year, I think. Two hunters been through town. First one ran off screaming into the desert. Last one was murdered but no one ever figured out by who. Whole town's edgy. Folks seein' shit that's not there or having nightmares. 'Sides that second hunter, we've only had one other murder. Mostly, folks just get into fights sometimes but never get to killin' each other."

Grimluk rubbed his jaw in thought. "Anything special about the town?"

"Not that I'm aware of. Greenreach Bluffs is just a lonely little mining town. For as long as I've been there, it's been a good town. After all this, and having to shut down the mine, I figured I needed come back out and find some new hunters. Maybe a whole posse, see if we can't take care of things that way."

"Sounds like a smart plan," Grimluk remarked.

"Though I doubt you'll get more than me. Even if someone else showed up, they might be skittish about the previous efforts."

"What about you, mister...?"

"Grimluk," the hunter said, extending his hand. Trilgor pumped it once. "Can't say I'm all that hesitant to take the job, though I should tell ya, I can't guarantee success. If I could, there'd be a lot less demons and a lot more peace. What I *can* guarantee is that I'll do my damnedest to kill this thing."

Trilgor leaned back, crossing his arms over his chest. He measured Grimluk. "Well, Grimluk, you certainly *look* like a tough bastard. I guess we'll see if that's bluster or truth. If you're amicable, I'd like to wait a few days before leaving, see if anymore hunters get out here."

"Sits well with me," Grimluk said.

Four days later, as the sun began to rise, the dregs of Border Rest went slinking back to their camps or rooms, drunk and likely relieved of all their coin. Grimluk stood on the porch of the Dancing Dwarf in the pale, rising light. The morning still warm with the heat of summer night. A little while later, Trilgor pushed through the bat-wing doors, greeting Grimluk with a yawn.

"I guess you're ready to go, eh? We can grab our horses and head out then. I got provisions last night."

"I don't ride."

"Pardon?"

"I walk. When need be, I run."

Trilgor looked at Grimluk dumbfounded. "You'll

walk? The Wastelands? Are you daft? You sure you're a demon hunter?"

"I trust my own feet to take me where I'm headed. Besides, this ain't my first time out there, I'll keep pace with your horse and I know what to expect. I'm heeled and still game to kill your demon."

The young man rubbed the back of his neck in thought for a moment. With a sigh, he nodded. "Yeah, alright. I'll grab my horse then and we'll be off."

Grimluk grunted in affirmation, following Trilgor to the livery. The stable master, a gray-haired halfling with a weasel's face, attempted to buy Trilgor's horse off of him. When Trilgor refused, he set to haggling over the bill. Trilgor groaned. Grimluk approached and sneered at the small man. He gulped hard and stopped haggling. Trilgor handed over a bilt and ten pennies. A young elf, probably no older than 40, brought the horse out, saddled and ready. The beast was strong and lean, covered in a fine, gray coat. Trilgor climbed into the saddle.

"She's a fine horse," Grimluk commented, petting her muzzle one with hand, and rubbing the groove of her chin with the other.

"Her name's Clementine, and she seems to like you. But you don't ride?"

"No."

Trilgor shrugged. "Let's be off then. We have about seven leagues to travel...are you sure you can't get a horse?"

Grimluk answered by heading off towards the edge of town and the true border to the Wastelands, which were marked by a long wooden fence, open at the road. Trilgor sighed, utterly sure the trip would not go well. He caught up to the hunter with ease and directed them into the Wastelands.

A few hours and a couple of leagues later, Trilgor shook his head in disbelief. "You weren't kidding about keeping pace," he said, unable to hide his surprise at Grimluk's ability to keep up with the horse's brisk trot.

He moved with long, quick strides with no signs of fatigue. "I been doin' this work a while."

The sun rose steadily into the sky. A few more hours would bring it into the noonday position. With each step, they could feel the heat rise up like a taunting spirit. Which made the occasional chill gust of wind all the more odd. Far from comforting, this chill went straight to the marrow. When the frozen wind would blow, punctuating the blistering heat with what felt like slices of ice, it kicked up dust and grit from the dead earth. The cold gusts made Trilgor feel like someone was stomping on his grave.

Clementine whinnied in protest as well, acting as if she would buck Trilgor and take off. If he couldn't control her, Grimluk would reach over to stroke her shoulder or neck. She would snort and begin to calm.

"I don't get it. You're so good with her but you don't ride," Trilgor remarked curiously.

"She knows what's out here. I imagine you had an easier ride in since you could run her more."

"I reckon so. Only took a few hours."

They continued on in silence. Off in the distance, all around them, the landscape seemed static. Rocks and dust and dead earth stretched on like a yawning, sun-soaked abyss. Their march had thus far been uneventful, merciless heat and frigid gusts aside. They both knew it wouldn't last. Trilgor had traveled unmolested the previous day only due to his horse's reliable speed. He knew he'd been lucky and now, they worked their way slowly towards the town, hoping that their luck would only run out marginally. A few dust-devils were preferable to something bigger.

Grimluk spoke their shared anxiety. "At the least, we're too far south and in the middle of too much rock for the worms to bother us."

Trilgor nodded in agreement before shooting the hunter a look of confusion. "Wait, worms?"

"Big ones," Grimluk responded with a grin.

Trilgor looked on bemused, waiting on him to continue.

"They'd eat the horse whole, or mostly whole. They don't seem to have any eyes so no one's quite sure how they hunt but they can't bust through solid rock. I killed one once. Took a stick of dynamite and a whole belt of ammo though."

"I've been out here for twelve years and I never heard of those. What else is out here?"

"You sure you wanna know?" Grimluk asked sincerely.

"I-," Trilgor caught himself. Did he want to know? He was traveling back to his home with a demon hunter, waiting for some unseen horror to make itself known. Did he really want to know about some of those horrors? "No," he finally spat.

Grimluk nodded. "So what's your story, eh? How'd you end up out here? Most folks aren't too keen on living out in the Wastelands."

"I'm captain of the Watchmen. Keep the peace,

handle anything that tries to get into the town. As for why I'm out here, well," Trilgor went quiet for a moment, gathering his thoughts. He reached up and rubbed his jaw in thought. "My parents were soldiers together. They fell in love, had me. There were some others that didn't much care for that. Chased us out of the southern territories. Da was human." Trilgor sighed. "He was killed protecting us.

"We ended up joining a caravan farther south that was headed up to Greenreach. Mom said she'd heard that Wasteland towns were always lookin' for workers. Peacekeepers or farmers, whatever was needed. Figured she could get on keepin' watch and we could relax for a while. Since she'd been a soldier, they made her Watch captain right away. Spent a few years training anyone who wanted to volunteer. Few more years keeping things runnin' smoothly.

"Then one evening a couple years back, a fuckin' bloodsucker shows up. He'd enthralled a whole caravan, figured he'd drain the town since we're so far out. Piece a shit killed her. She was tough as nails though and surprised him. He'd latched on and started draining her during a guard switch but instead of just falling away, she grabbed a hold and held on to the damn thing till we could stake it. Mayor figured I was a good replacement."

Grimluk walked without reply for a few minutes. "Your mother sounds like she was one amazing woman."

"She was. She use to tease dad sometimes too. Said I got her good looks but his brains." Trilgor smiled fondly at the memory.

"Well, we are a good lookin' people," Grimluk replied with a laugh. "I'm surprised you ended up out here, though. There are plenty of villages in the southern territories that would've taken your family in. Your mother's home village surely would have welcomed you home."

"Da asked her about that once. She said she had...what was it...been an exception to her family's legacy. Never would tell us what that meant, just that we couldn't go back."

"I see."

"We should probably take lunch. Clementine could use some water and my gut's rumblin'."

"Water her. I'll keep watch." Far in the distance, Grimluk saw something huge lumber behind a copse of decaying trees.

The sun hung low in the sky, shining bright with the light of the coming dusk. Orange and red had started coloring the horizon and the dust of the day covered the travelers and the horse. After six leagues baking in the sun and the Wastelands' shadeless miles and frozen wind, they had made it to the entrance of the valley that housed Greenreach Bluffs. The land began to slope and dip. A thousand years earlier, the valley had been a shallow lake. Now it was desert hardpan. Miles in the distance, Grimluk could just make out the cliffs that made up the border of the valley.

"How far we got?" Grimluk asked.

"Bout a league or so. Back of the valley."

Grimluk grunted.

Some distance away, as the pair continued onward, the earth and dust began to stir. It started gently, like a drunkard still too inebriated to get up from where they fell the night before. The ice-wind blew and bit Grimluk and Trilgor once more. And then it stopped. There was no fade in the gust, it merely stopped immediately.

The ground stirred more heavily. Rotting eyes began to open. Bony fingers grasped the ground as leathery hands pushed up. Arms, heads, and bodies rose slowly up out of the valley floor, another form of perverse flora. The Wastelands were teeming with death, decay, and bizarre and ghastly creatures.

Up they rose, focusing their faintly glowing eyes (or sockets in some cases) on the travelers. Low groans escaped broken, rotting jaws. Teeth clacked together as the ghouls tried to bite prey that still had distance from them. The ones already on their feet began to shamble towards their would-be meals

Grimluk growled in annoyance. "I hate ghouls. They're so...tedious."

"Deal with them often?" Trilgor responded, surprised and a little amused.

"More than I'd like," Grimluk replied dryly as he pulled his revolver from its holster. "A few years ago, I had to reinforce the butt of my pistol. Almost shattered from one too many brain-bashes."

As one of the ghouls neared, Grimluk stepped forward and brought the pistol down into its putrid head. The skull shattered like brittle glass under his swing. Brain and rancid blood spit out from the sides and back. Each one that followed the first met the same fate. Trilgor sat behind and watched, still a bit stunned at the hunter's nonchalance. Ahead of Grimluk, more corpses shambled forward as more yet rose from the dirt and their slumber.

"This is why I hate the walking dead," Grimluk said loudly for his companion to hear. "There's never just a few." He caved in the skull of another and watched as it sank down. The faint green glow in its eyes disappeared. "No, you see a few and there's really a dozen or more."

"I've never really had to deal with them. The town magician makes sure the dead stay in their graves. I guess I was riding too fast to notice these assholes." Grimluk grunted loudly. Trilgor was unsure whether that was his reply or just the sound he'd made before bringing down another ghoul.

"Not many folks know it but ghouls are reanimated by demons," Grimluk said, cracking a new ghoul square in the forehead.

"That right?"

"They like to crawl into graveyards and lonely places, find corpses that haven't been tended to properly. You can see the results." Grimluk swiped at another ghoul as it approached.

"So if they're demons, why do they go down so easily when you smash their heads?"

"Ya know," another ghoul crumpled to the ground, "I'm not entirely sure. I think it might be something to do with the brain, but I've never looked into it. There's probably a wizard or another hunter out there that knows."

"Hm, well, at least this seems to be all we have to deal with," Trilgor remarked as he unsheathed his saber. "I'm ready to get home." He sliced through an approaching ghoul's skull.

The bone-chilling wind that had plagued them

returned. It began to encircle them, biting sharply. An eerie, disembodied laugh echoed in the air around them. The wind left then, moving faster than it should have, taking off behind them. Grimluk turned and walked a few feet towards where they'd come from.

"Town's at the back of the valley, right?"

"Yeah, why?"

"I think something heard you."

Trilgor split the skull of the nearest ghoul before turning the horse around and joining Grimluk, who was currently pulling a black bandanna out of his coat pocket and tying it around his face. Rushing towards them, a few hundred yards away, was a wall of dust.

"If I was you, I'd get goin'," Grimluk suggested.

"And just leave you to the storm and the ghouls?"

"I told ya, I been at this a while. Better that thing focuses on me than you. I'll make it."

"With all due respect, fuck no."

Grimluk sighed. "Fine. Hit the ghouls and try to stick close. When that wall hits, it's gonna hit hard, and the things that made it like getting people lost. Seems to be the favored activity of pesky spirits that can't do more than annoy."

The pair returned to the task of whittling down the number of ghouls currently groaning and pawing for their flesh. Grimluk led the pair, doing his best to work quickly. Trilgor split and stabbed any skull that got within his blade's reach. Each second they spent on the shambling corpses, the storm advanced, whipping up every ounce of dust and grit in its path.

They managed to get the ghouls' numbers down

to a dozen before the storm hit. Grimluk hadn't been exaggerating, Trilgor reflected. If he'd been a smaller man, the storm might have toppled him right off the horse. He looked to his left, trying to keep an eye on Grimluk but within moments, the storm had brought a coarse darkness. Trilgor couldn't even see his arms past his elbow. The sound of the wind was a roar in the young captain's ears.

"Go!" roared Grimluk from somewhere in the dark. "Go!"

Against his better judgment, Trilgor pushed the horse into a gallop and took off towards Greenreach Bluffs.

CHAPTER 2

Grimluk walked through the storm, swathed in dust and cloaked in the darkness it brought. Several yards ahead of him lay the town's entrance, where the storm lessened as the spirits within collided with a rippling energy surrounding the town. Dust rained harmlessly down as it was robbed of its momentum. Two human Watchmen on duty, a man and a woman. Grimluk walked slowly towards them startling them as he emerged into the flickering energy's light like a pale phantom, covered from head to toe with a thick coating of dust.

He stopped as they pointed their rifles at him, holding up his hands, allowing the Watchmen to observe him, letting them know he was real and awaited their response. The crackling energy repelling the spirits fizzed and popped, casting light over the three of them while the dust swirled around Grimluk.

"Charlie, you see this too?" the Watchman on the right asked the Watchman on the left.

"Big fucker covered in dust," Charlie remarked.

"Ayup. We both see him them. Reckon we should ask what he wants." He stepped forward, holding a rifle, and shouted at Grimluk. "We both see ya, so you're real. Step close and state your business!"

Grimluk moved closer, still holding his hands up, slowly reaching over to pull the bandanna from his face, revealing the still-green skin beneath, now quickly being covered by the dust. "I was hired to fix your demon problem," he said shouted over the howling wind.

The Watchman looked back at his peer before turning back to the green-skinned wanderer. "How do we know you're really a hunter? How do we know you ain't a bandit?"

Grimluk stepped closer still, getting right up near the magical barrier surrounding the town, the energy rippling at his approach. He reached out slowly with his left hand and touched the barrier. It crackled and shimmered like a soap bubble, humming lightly in resistance to Grimluk's hand. The Watchmen looked on, curiosity and suspicion covering their faces. Grimluk pushed his hand through the barrier.

Charlie's rifle was up against her shoulder and aimed squarely at his head in an instant. "Hold back, orc!" she shouted. Grimluk pulled his left hand back from the barrier, holding it back up in continued effort to show he was peaceful.

"Yeah, okay...you're true," the other Watchman said.

The trio stood silently for a few moments before Grimluk spoke again. "Would it set you at ease to know that I was traveling with your captain?"

Charlie looked over at her partner and back. "Trilgor? What do you know about the captain?"

Grimluk cleared his throat and reported to the Watchmen what had transpired as the two had traveled together.

"That certainly explains the big-ass dust storm, don't it, Peter," Charlie remarked.

"Yeah. Put your rifle down, Char," Peter said, still looking at Grimluk. "Trilgor arrived a few hours ago. And in worse shape than you appear to be in for someone attacked by ghouls and blasted by a dust storm. If you speak true, that means I could go ask him 'bout the big fuckin' orc wantin' to come in town, yeah?"

"That's right," Grimluk replied. Something screeched in the distance, long and half-muted.

Peter worked his jaw in thought for a moment. "Yeah, alright, we'll let ya in. Mind yourself though."

Charlie remained silent, watching Grimluk with suspicion as she slung her rifle back over her shoulder. The pair motioned for him to come through. The barrier buzzed and crackled, trembling as Grimluk slipped through quickly. The spirits howled as they bounced off the barrier, angry that the two travelers had escaped them. The sound was sudden and close and made the Watchmen jump. The dust storm dissipated, leaving the town covered by a hazy shadow.

"What happened to Trilgor?" Grimluk asked, as he endeavored to beat some of the dust loose off himself. It fell away in great showers, piling up at his feet.

"He come in barely hangin' on to his horse," Charlie answered. "We made sure it was really him and got him back into the bunkhouse. He should be there resting."

"Thank you," Grimluk replied, removing his hat, revealing a mostly shaved head with a strip of black hair down the center that came to a point at the base of his skull. The dust dumped from his hat, joining the rest of the pile.

"Yeah, sure," Charlie responded dryly, waving away some of the grit.

"Just head in, you can see the Watch from here," Peter said. Grimluk nodded to the man, moving on towards the town proper, settling his hat back on his head.

Greenreach Bluffs was split into two areas, separated by stone walls a little taller than Grimluk, behind which he could see a very large, tall building. The town as a whole was shaped in a rough hexagon. The area between the inner and outer walls housed the town's farm and livestock pens. The ground in the outer ring was still green and alive with grass, though it was yellowing slightly. Grimluk wondered if the barrier helped combat the effects of the Wastelands.

The farm sat to his left. There were a few fruit trees, mostly apples and some lemons while vegetables grew in stone planters. He could see a small greenhouse at the very back. To his right, the livestock pens housed a large herd of goats, several chicken coops, and a very small herd of shaggy cattle. The space was wide and accommodated its respective facilities comfortably. Grimluk crossed the long yard and passed through the inner wall.

To his immediate left was a big, stone well. To his right was the livery, sparsely used as it was. As he passed by, he saw Trilgor's horse. He was glad Clementine had returned safely with her rider. Following the inner wall from the livery was the Watchmen training yard, which fed into the Watch house itself. The building ran the entirety of its section of the inner wall, housing a small cell block, an armory, a mess hall, and the barracks for the full-time volunteers.

Grimluk made his way briskly to the Watch. A pair of women, a human and a halfling, sat out on the porch around a small table watching the sky. Both had dirty blonde hair. They wore what basically constituted the uniform for the Watchmen; boots, dark trousers, work shirts, and vests. Each wore a plain leather gun belt that shone with the brass of cartridges at home in their loops.

Grimluk approached. "Pardon, friends," he said, touching the brim of his hat.

"Yeah?" the halfling woman responded warily.

"My name is Grimluk. I'm looking for Trilgor."

"Josie," the human woman said. "This is Sam. What for?" Josie inquired a touch sharply.

"He hired me for a job. We were traveling here together when we were separated by the dust storm."

Sam looked him up and down before holding his gaze. Josie wrinkled her nose at him. She pulled out a little cloth pouch and set about rolling herself a cigarette. "So you're the new hunter, huh?"

"That's right."

"Well shit. You wanna take him, or you want me to?" Sam asked.

"Hop on it," Josie replied dryly.

Sam hopped down from her chair and motioned for Grimluk to follow her. The inside of the Watch was sparse and practical but supplied a few comforts for the full-timers, who got their own bunk room and their own beds. Sam led him through the mess hall, back into the barracks. Grimluk could see Trilgor in the back corner, sitting up in his bed.

"Hey, Cap, this orc says he's here to see you."

"Fuck me, you actually made it," Trilgor blurted out. "Thanks, Sam." She headed back for the front porch and Josie, taking a moment to eye Grimluk before she left.

"I told ya I'd done this before," Grimluk responded casually. "You seem like you made it alright."

"Yeah...just got lost in the dark. Still not sure what happened. Storm hit, things went dark. Think I trampled a ghoul when we bolted. Somehow, Clementine got me back here. That horse is somethin' else."

"That she is."

"Well, now that you're here, I guess I should see about gettin' you settled at the Sliver now. Then we can go see Selbie. He's gonna wanna meet you."

"I'm ready when you are."

The Silver Sliver sat in the middle of town, forming a small group with the two other establishments of the town, the general store and the blacksmith. The foundation of the Sliver was stone, while the body was mostly wood with some stone walling. The windows were dirty and speckled with grit and bits of ash that would float over from the blacksmith's forge. Trilgor opened the thick ironwood door, imported like the rest of the town's wood supply, and led Grimluk inside, the hunter ducking his head slightly as he entered. The place was dead silent. Aside from Trilgor and himself, there were only two other people to be seen; the owner, who stood behind the bar, and an old halfling playing alone with a deck of cards.

The bar stood to the right. Behind it stood a mirrored wall and cabinetry lined up with various bottles of alcohol. A doorway at the other end led to a small kitchen that sat behind the wall of booze. To the left was a large room filled with tables. Some were round and plain, for drinking and supping. Others were covered in dark-blue or faded green felt for card playing. They sat placidly with cards and chips stacked in their centers, a thin layer of dust had settled from disuse. The man with the cards ignored them, never looking up from his game.

"Mattias," Trilgor called, approaching the bar.

The balding, middle-aged man turned to face the pair. His face was a little dirty and what remaining hair he had was tied back, hanging loosely between his shoulders. Muddy brown eyes took in the sight of Grimluk. Mostly, they were tired but now, locked onto the hunter, apprehension flowed out of them.

"What can I do for ya, Captain?" Mattias answered. His eyes only left Grimluk for a moment.

"This is Grimluk. He'll be needin' a room for the foreseeable future."

"Got plenty a rooms. And a fair price for any friend a yours." An uncomfortable smile spread across Mattias's face.

"The man's here to kill our demon. I think you can let him stay as part of his compensation."

The smile ceased to be. "No, I will *not*. I got a business to run, demon hunter or not, and aside from old Edgar there, who *you* are paying for, I don't exactly get many patrons lately."

Trilgor started to argue but Grimluk put a hand on his shoulder. "I can pay," he said. "If you've got a nice brew, I'm a bit parched from the dust. If you got any tankards to fit me, I'll take one of those, if not, two of whatever you brew."

Mattias stared at Grimluk for a moment, a battle playing across his face. He didn't really like the hunter, and didn't currently care for Trilgor either but understood the young man kept the town reasonably safe. His desire for coin won out. "Yeah, ten pennies for the two. Twenty gets ya a biscuit and beans too."

Grimluk produced a bilt, setting it flat on the bar top. "Just the beer for now."

"I don't make change, hunter."

"Didn't ask for change."

Mattias wondered what Grimluk's angle was but shrugged, sliding the coin into his pocket, and silently served his new guest. He set the tankards down. Grimluk took one and began downing it, clinking it back down a moment later. He wiped his mouth across the back of his hand, and then picked up the other one which disappeared just as quickly. Despite his very prominent tusks, he never spilled a drop. He let out a sigh of relief.

"Thanks," Grimluk said before belching. "Fair bit better than whatever they sell in Border Rest."

Mattias, arms crossed and face smudged in annoyance, waved his index finger in curt reply. Trilgor frowned before readdressing the matter of Grimluk's accommodations.

"Alright, so he'll pay ya for the room. I'm takin' him to see Selbie now. Have the room ready when he gets back and set up a tab."

"Fine, fine, stop bein' so bossy. I ain't one a yer Watchmen."

It was Grimluk's turn to frown now. "Here, a down payment for the room," he said, cutting the tension between the two men. He set a one, glittering gold glut down on the bar top and thought Mattias's eyes would pop out of his head. He turned back to Trilgor. "Lead the way."

Trilgor laughed and led Grimluk back outside. The pair stood on the Sliver's porch looking around the town for a moment. "I'm sorry for Mattias. I'd say that'd be to blame on what's happened around here but he's always been a bit of a greedy ass."

Grimluk grunted in a way that said it didn't matter. "What's the mayor like?" he asked instead.

Trilgor thought about the question for a moment. "Old man. Was in charge when we got here. He seemed pretty stand-up, amiable and always talked like he wanted the best for the town. This whole mess has hit him too though. He fought with the last hunter a lot. He rarely leaves his house these days."

"Mm," was all Grimluk replied.

Trilgor stepped off the porch and headed for the mayor's big house, which sat against the leftmost side of the bluffs that made up the back of the town, behind a short, stone wall topped with a small, iron fence, and an iron gate. Grimluk followed him down the empty street. The dull haze from the storm had grown thinner, letting more light back into the town. Grimluk didn't see anyone else as they walked.

"Not much to the town, really," Trilgor said. "You've seen the Watch, the Sliver, the smith and the store. Over here's the magician's temple and the mayor's house." As the pair reached the gate of the mayor's house, he turned and pointed behind the Sliver. "Back there's the mine."

"I guess that means the other big building is

apartments then."

"It is. That's the grand tour."

A big gust of wind blew through the town, sweeping down from the bluff behind the house. It kicked up several dust devils and with several more gusts, they spun harmlessly through the center of the town. Trilgor unlatched and pushed through the gate as another gust threatened to take Grimluk's hat off.

The courtyard was pitiful. Dry, overgrown grass jutted out of planters with the occasional, sickly-looking group of flowers. The purple petals of one flower in particular could be pretty in the right season but in their current state, looked more like leaves made of dried blood.

The house was built in similar fashion to the Silver Sliver. It started in stone and peaked in wood. The foundation was much bigger, appearing to have been built up from a basement or cellar. It was three stories in all and, like the Sliver, had an ironwood door as well, though much more ornately carved.

A small set of stone steps led up to a wooden porch. The orcs stepped up to the door and Trilgor gave two, solid thumps with his fist. After a minute or two, the door ripped open. There stood a halfling woman, red-haired, hazel-eyed, glaring up at him.

"You ruined my soufflé, you jackass!"

It caught Trilgor off guard. "I'm sorry, Sadie. How was I supposed to know?"

"What on Arkod do you want, comin' up and bangin' on doors like you're comin' through?"

Grimluk stood there a moment, surprised at the ferocity of the tiny woman and her anger at the ruined dessert.

"I need to speak with Selbie," the young captain said with a sigh. "I found a new hunter." He motioned towards Grimluk.

He touched the brim of his hat. "Hullo, miss."

Sadie looked him up and down, like she was sizing him up. Then, without warning, she slammed the door in their faces. They stood there, unsure of what just happened, and waited.

"Is she always like this?" Grimluk asked Trilgor.

"Yes, actually. Whatever issues Sadie's suffered, she's one of a few who hides it well."

The door ripped open again as he finished speaking. This time, an older man with graying hair and round spectacles stood next to the irate baker. "Here are the dummies," she almost hissed before she disappeared back into the house.

Grimluk grinned to himself. He couldn't recall anyone ever calling him a dummy, much less someone small enough he could pick up and toss with one arm.

"Ah, I'm sorry about that. You know how seriously Sadie takes her baking," the old man said. "Bring your guest in, Captain. I understand we have a lot to discuss."

Trilgor motioned for the hunter to enter. Grimluk nodded and stepped his hulking form through the door. Trilgor followed and closed it. The mayor reached out towards the hunter. "Kenton Selbie, Mayor of Greenreach Bluffs."

"Grimluk," he said, shaking his host's hand.

"I suppose we should have a seat and get right to it then. This way," Selbie said, leading Grimluk into a large sitting room full of leather furniture. He motioned for his guests to take a seat, doing so as well. Grimluk elected to stand, reminding the mayor that he was still covered in the storm's dust. Trilgor sat down on the matching couch. Selbie sat in his favorite chair; an upholstered clawfoot of dark earth tones.

"Sadie," Selbie called out, "would you kindly brew some tea? Would you gentlemen care for anything?"

Grimluk waved two fingers in the air dismissively. Trilgor shook his head.

"Now then, just for my own piece of mind, Captain Trilgor told you about the previous hunters, correct?" Grimluk nodded. "That's good. Don't want you walkin' in blind, now do we?"

"It's helped a time or two," Grimluk remarked a touch dryly.

"And can I assume he told you how bad things are?"

"He did. Fights, hallucinations, murder. First hunter ran screaming into the Wastelands. Second dead by someone's hand. What else do I need to know?"

"Folks round here probably aren't gonna have too much trust in you doin' your job," Selbie said casually.

"With two failed hunters, I'd expect so."

"That's good you don't take it personally. Folks might say some nasty things to you as well."

"Sir," Trilgor spoke up, "I'd really like to call a town meeting and introduce Grimluk to everyone. I'm sure some of them know he's here but most everyone just hides away now. It might set everyone at ease."

The mayor nodded. "That might be a good idea. Might be a good test for our new hunter. Go ahead and set it up for tomorrow afternoon."

"That alright with you?" Trilgor asked Grimluk.

"It is."

"Excellent, excellent," Selbie said. "Have you set him up with accommodations yet?"

"Mattias didn't agree to arrangements previously used. Our new friend went ahead and paid him for a room and for drink as a good faith showing."

"It's only money," Grimluk said idly.

Selbie sat quietly for a moment with his hands clasped against his chest. Sadie came in with a cup of tea and handed it to him, giving the orcs a foul look as she left. "Well, I suppose there's no need to speak to him on the matter then. Do you require anything else, Mr. Grimluk?"

"At the moment, just knowing more about what's been going on here and to know when I'll be able to interview the townsfolk. To best figure out the nature of your beast, I'll need to gather as much information as I can. It probably has a lair nearby too. Maybe even in the town."

"As I told ya in Border Rest, people see things and have gotten violent and mistrusting. We didn't even completely know what was happening until a week or so before Negos atta-"

The mayor interrupted. "That's enough for now, Trilgor. We need to have the town meeting first. Let everyone decide if they want his help."

Trilgor sat momentarily stunned. Grimluk frowned but remained silent. "So we're done til tomorrow then?" Trilgor was more than a little curt.

"Yes, though you might want to have the Watchmen inform the town of the meeting." The mayor's face was the very image of polite. "I appreciate your understanding, Mr. Grimluk. I'm sure we'll get this all sorted out tomorrow."

Trilgor and the mayor stood once more. Trilgor quickly made his way out, all but tearing the door off its hinges in his haste. Grimluk tipped his hat to Mayor Selbie and again to Sadie as she appeared in the hallway. The door closed gently behind him. Sadie stood quietly for a moment before addressing the mayor.

"This town barely knows what's good for itself anymore and you wanna let it vote on gettin' rid of the gods damned demon plaguin' it?"

Selbie's face grew stern. He ignored her question and headed up the stairs to his study. Sadie sighed and wandered back to the kitchen where she grabbed a small bottle of brandy and poured herself a glass. "Asshole."

Grimluk found Trilgor waiting for him at the iron gate, fuming at the abrupt end of their meeting. "Given just what little you'd told me," he said as he approached, "that was to be expected."

Trilgor opened the gate and stepped over the threshold, Grimluk following behind. He stood next to the frustrated young man. They stood quietly in evening sun, which sat just above the cliff-face at the far end of the valley, casting a fuzzy orange glow through the remaining bits of dust billowing about.

"Come on, I'll buy you a drink. You can tell me some more about your mother."

"Yeah...alright," the young captain said with a

sigh.

The next day, the town began gathering outside the Silver Sliver. Despite mostly shutting themselves away after the mine shut down, the prospect of something to do piqued the townsfolk's interest. Mayor Selbie was there to greet folks as they arrived. Grimluk stood on the porch of the Sliver staring out at distrustful faces. The skies had turned gray. Off in the distance, dark clouds rolled and threatened rain.

A chorus of chatter washed through the town's center. They questioned each other. Who was he? Who let him in? How did he make it through the dust storm? Some made bets on how long he'd last. Others wondered about their safety with a hunter in town. The whole town was nothing but cynicism. Finally, the mayor called for attention.

"Friends, I thank you for joining us today. As you know, we have a guest in town and a decision to make regarding him. For close to a year now, we've dealt with certain issues of demonic activity. Two hunters have visited us, claiming the power to right our wrongs. Both failed. Now we have a new...hero. Captain Trilgor brought him here and after a discussion with them, I would put it to you. I will let him speak to you. After we've all had a chance to question him, we'll make a decision." The mayor motioned for Grimluk to step forward and address the crowd before he stepped away to join it.

Grimluk squared up and took his place in front of the townsfolk. "My name is Grimluk. I am a demon hunter. Ask of me what you will and I will answer to the best of my ability." For a little added emphasis, he pushed the brim of his hat up, taking away the shadow that usually cloaked his eyes. For what seemed like hours, the gathered mass remained silent as he studied them. The quiet sat over them like an uncomfortable blanket. People shuffled and fidgeted and coughed, wanting to call this would-be savior out but, strangely, being too afraid.

"What kind of experience you got?" a voice finally piped up.

"Charlie, correct?" She nodded. "On my hat band sit thirteen teeth from thirteen demons. My first kills. Each one was an arduous trial and a test as I trained as an apprentice. We don't take the training lightly. Those of us who take up the mantle go through brutal ordeals and intense study to prepare us for hunting in the world at large. Hunters bring back the knowledge they've gained in their travels and share it freely. We learn about different types of demons, different ways to discover and kill them. It all builds through thirteen demons, final tests as we learn, and each of those tests ends with death. The demon's or yours if you're not careful. I slew my thirteen and slain dozens since."

Charlie's mouth fell agape at that. The crowd murmured in reply. As it quieted, another voice spoke up. "How would you kill the demon?"

"Have you or anyone else seen it?" Grimluk asked, scanning the faces.

The speaker, an elf woman, looked around before shaking her head, along with several others.

"Then I don't know." Loud murmurs met Grimluk's reply. He spoke up to continue his answer. "If you haven't seen it, then I don't know what kind of demon is causing your problems or even how strong it is. Could be that the only thing I've got to do to send it back to the Abyss is find it and put a bullet it in its head. Could be I'll have to find its lair and whatever's keeping it anchored to the world and destroy that. I won't know unless I investigate."

"What kinda plan you got?" came another member of the throng.

"Explore the town, the area, the mine. Interview those willing. Children and adult alike. I'll need as much information as I can get."

"And why should we involve the children at all?" Mayor Selbie asked. "The children have been through enough without some outsider badgering them."

Grimluk stared hard into the mayor's eyes. He held his gaze long enough to make the man start to squirm. "Because the children will speak plainly about themselves. The parents might distort their experiences out of fear or dismissal."

A fidgeting silence blanketed the crowd once more. Thunder rolled in the distance. A small commotion broke the silence as Sadie pushed through to the front of the crowd to ask the hunter a question. "Why should we trust you though?"

Grimluk crossed his arms and looked at her. Sadie's face was plain and it was easy to see the question bore no malice. "The best thing I can say to that is the same thing I told Trilgor when I met him at Border Rest. I can't guarantee I'll succeed, but I guarantee that I'll give it everything I've got. And if it turns out it kills me, then Death'll take two that day. I can offer no more and no less."

Sadie seemed satisfied at this answer. The crowd grew in noise again as the people talked among themselves. Mayor Selbie frowned before speaking up again. "If you can really help, I think, and I'm sure the rest of the town would agree, that a demonstration of your abilities might be warranted. Some proof that you're not just some imbecile that knows a little about demons."

Grimluk worked his jaw in thought. Several members of the town voiced their agreement with the mayor. "Name your terms," he finally replied. His eyes bore a hole through Selbie once again.

"Yes, I-we would like to see what you're capable of. Just leave it to me, I'll make the arrangements. And," he said, momentarily looking back at the storm rolling in, "weather permitting, how does tomorrow afternoon sound? Do you find this agreeable?"

"I do," Grimluk grunted. "Am I allowed to know the details of this...demonstration prior to the time?"

"I think it would best showcase your talents if things were a surprise, don't you?"

"I reckon so."

Thunder rolled overhead as the crowd began to disperse. The clouds had grown darker. Most of them were pleased with the mayor's call for a test. As the town's center thinned out, Trilgor approached Grimluk. "You okay with how things turned out?"

"Went pretty much like I expected. I've got an extra day to prepare though. It'll rain soon."

"I wish I knew what he was up to," Trilgor said with a sigh.

"We'll learn soon enough," Grimluk replied, patting Trilgor's shoulder.

An hour later, Grimluk sat in his room at the Silver Sliver, contemplating what was to come. The rain started slowly, a few drops pattering against the window at first, before the clouds released all at once, pelting the glass with a soft fury. The ground soaked it up, as a sullen quiet settled over Greenreach Bluffs.

CHAPTER 3

The room was Mattias's smallest. To the left of the door was the bed. The linens were comfortable enough but Grimluk's feet pushed up against the footboard. He made due sleeping on his side. The window was tall and less broad than he was. In the dull light of the clouded morning, he could see the grit that speckled the outside. Too ingrained to be washed away in the rain now. He could see the blacksmith's shop across the way. The forge was quiet in the rain. To the right of the window, and pushed into the corner, was a square, wooden table, with two chairs on either open side. His bag and gun belt sat in a heap on it while his coat hung over the top rail of the chair closest to the window with his hat drooping from the finial.

The rain had tapered off an hour or so after sunrise before finally giving up. The clouds hung in the air, bereft of their cargo and soundless once more. Grimluk stood at the window, gazing out, lost in thought. He was frustrated. Frustrated at this little test and being kept from working til it was over. Or at least, most of the work. As he'd seen it, the Sliver was empty, save Mattias, his son (who ran things at night), and Edgar, who had still been playing his card game last night. Grimluk wondered if he could try to talk to the old man and hoped maybe someone else would wander in as well.

As he gazed out into the rainy street, he saw a dwarf come around the far corner of the Sliver, dressed in dirty, brown overalls that seemed to be dripping with mud from the rain. Streaks of mud covered the dwarf's olive face as well, almost resembling warpaint, but the dwarf hardly seemed to notice.

What he did notice was Grimluk standing at the window, and at first, visibly attempted to ignore him. He seemed unable to ignore Grimluk, however, finally stopping to stare at the hunter before turning around quickly and heading back the way he'd come. Grimluk's throat rumbled in thought.

A few hours later, around noon and after a late, heavy breakfast of meat, eggs, and potatoes, Grimluk sat in silence at a table near the door. The only sounds were Mattias half-snoring behind the bar and the soft flap of Edgar's cards. Mattias had put a little rocking chair behind the bar, near the front wall, out of the way and sat dozing. Mattias snorted loudly, his boots scuffing the floor as he startled awake. Grimluk turned towards Edgar, watching him for a moment. He decided to try and speak to the old halfling.

"May I join you?" he asked as he approached. Edgar remained silent, continuing to flip his cards. Grimluk pulled out a chair. "I'm Grimluk."

Edgar sighed, gathering up his cards. Nimble fingers shuffled the deck anew and then laid them out in a new game. Grimluk wasn't sure what the game was. He watched Edgar play for a minute but couldn't discern the goal.

"I'm not sure if you heard but I'm the new demon hunter. I was hoping-" Grimluk stopped speaking for a moment. Edgar's hands had begun to move faster as he spoke. "I was hoping maybe we could talk about how you've been through everything." Edgar responded with a grunt of frustration before shuffling the cards again.

Grimluk opened his mouth to speak again but Edgar stopped him with a sudden screech. Mattias jerked up to his feet with a yelp. Grimluk nodded and left the old man to his cards. He returned to his previous table and wondered if anyone else would come in.

A little while later, a halfling pushed his way in, working his small frame against the heavy door. He was chubby and ruddy-cheeked, dressed in a simple, uncolored shirt with the sleeves rolled up and dark brown trousers. Chestnut hair flopped about in thick waves, and, as was usual for his people, his feet were bare and covered in a thick hair. His eyes were big and honey-colored. Deep bags hung under them.

The halfling happened to look towards Grimluk as he got the door shut and froze for a moment. Grimluk offered a smile and a nod. The poor man jumped a little, surprised at both the hunter's presence and the friendly gesture. He lifted a hand to wave lightly before he turned quickly and shouted for Mattias. His voice squeaked, causing him to jump again out of embarrassment.

"Uh, Mattias," he said again, trying to keep his voice from climbing.

The old man yawned and stood up, leaning over the bar top. "What, Thomas?" He looked somewhere between bored and annoyed with the halfling.

"I'll have a pint." Thomas reached up to put his pennies on the bar. A moment later, he was taking the tankard from Mattias's hands and turning around to pick his seat. Grimluk was staring at him.

Grimluk motioned for Thomas to join him. "It's been far too quiet around here."

Thomas hesitated for a long moment. Maybe several long moments. He decided if Grimluk meant him any harm, he'd already be hurting. No sense in letting his ale go flat while he worried. He set his pint down and hopped in the chair to Grimluk's left. They sat in a thick silence for a few minutes before Thomas spoke.

"You're the demon hunter."

"I am."

"I'm Thomas." He extended his hand more out of habit than anything else.

Grimluk took the halfling's hand firmly between his fingers and gave it a light shake. "Grimluk."

"Do...do you really think you can help?"

"If I'm allowed. You were there at the meeting yesterday, right?"

"For most of it..."

"For all I know, the 'demonstration' will be someone putting a bullet in me." Grimluk took a gulp from one of his tankards, his words hanging in the air momentarily.

Thomas thought that seemed morbidly casual. "And what if it is?"

"Maybe I'm bulletproof," he said with a grin. "Would your mayor do that?"

Thomas thought earnestly on the question, gulping down some of his ale as he did so. "No. I don't believe he would." Grimluk nodded lightly in response. Thomas looked at Grimluk, an expression of worry painted across his face.

"I've never seen a halfling make that kind of face before." An air of jest hung on his words.

"I've been wondering a couple things. I heard someone say orcs are the best demon hunters. Is that true?"

"Sometimes," Grimluk replied with a shrug. "I think we certainly take to it easier than most folks. We have a certain," he stopped for a moment, licking a tusk in thought, "a certain intimacy with the evils that infect our world."

"Because you were evil once?" Thomas grimaced slightly as Grimluk sighed. He had upset the orc and now he would be squashed.

"I know what the old stories say but we weren't evil."

"I'm sorry, I didn't mean-," Thomas started to say before Grimluk waved him off.

"Don't worry about it. We'll skip the Orcish history lesson. What else were you wondering?"

"Oh, well," Thomas mulled the question over for a moment trying to decide if he really wanted to ask. "Just what exactly *is* the Abyss?"

"Well, no one knows exactly for sure but we've heard demons mention it, like it's where they're from or where they go if they're banished from our world. From what I've learned, it's a pretty ugly place."

"Oh..."

"How bout I buy you another pint if you want and you can tell me how you've been faring since the demon showed up?" Grimluk offered.

"I thought you weren't allowed to talk to us yet?"

"Not yet, no. And that's why I'm going to listen," Grimluk said with a wink. A grin tugged at Thomas's cheek as Grimluk got up to get more beer from the dozing Mattias. Thomas swallowed hard and finished his pint.

A few moments later, Grimluk clunked a meaty fistful of tankards down on the table, and slid one towards his new acquaintance. Thomas grabbed it tentatively with both hands, staring down into the foam, watching it bubble while he thought about his story.

"I guess the best place to start is to say that I never had any sleep problems before all this. Occasionally, you eat somethin' that don't sit well and you have a weird dream but that's normal. Natural even, right? I didn't even notice the dreams at first. Figured it was just somethin' I ate. Shrugged 'em off. Now..." He downed half his pint and belched. "It's like the world goes wrong. Sometimes I see things while it's happening but mostly, it feels like reality's been pulled inside-out and gone tipsy. Everything, and I mean everything, goes far away but not, you get me? The whole world skinny, stretches leagues away. It's all still close enough to touch though. And touching, oh gods." A small moan escaped Thomas's throat.

"The size of things goes wrong. If you were near when I had one of these, you'd be my size but you'd be so much bigger too. Like you'd shrunk but grown to the heavens all at once. All wrong. And everything feels that way. A splinter feels as big as the biggest tree. A pebble would sit in my hand and feel like I was holding a mountain. The only thing that seemed to fight it off is light. So I'd light my lamp back up. Or try to. Some nights, it's all too much and...and...I just lay there. I use to scream at it. The madness of it.

"It's all worse now though. I avoid the bed but that's just making it worse. I said I see things sometimes and I do and the things are worse in the dreams. Sometimes, I feel like something's watching me and then I'll see glowing eyes. Just the eyes. Or some sort of light. Sometimes, when everything stretches out to eternity, I can see...gods damn it, I don't know, *things*. I don't know what to call them but things. I can see them in the dark edges of everything and they don't make sense but I know they're alive."

Moments of silence drifted by before Thomas sighed heavily. "Fuck," he croaked. "It's so much worse than I thought. Sayin' it all like that, out loud." He swallowed hard and for a moment, it looked like he would start crying.

Grimluk remained silent. He wanted to let Thomas catch his breath. Everything had tumbled out of the man like the rush from a broken dam. He watched Thomas lay his head down against the table and suck in a deep breath. The Sliver stood silent save for the sound Edgar's cards and Mattias's light snoring coming from behind the bar. Grimluk and Thomas sat in the quiet and drank their ale.

"Thank you," Grimluk said when he felt Thomas had calmed down.

Thomas nodded absently, staring ahead in a half-daze. "I hope you can beat the test. I hope you can help us."

Grimluk grunted in agreement. The afternoon rolled on in quiet contemplation. By late evening, Thomas and the gray skies had returned where they'd come from. The ground had already begun to dry in the heat of the day and the sun's reappearance only hastened the evaporation. The test would happen the next day for sure. Grimluk would be prepared. It was his job to be prepared.

The rain had done little to quell the heat. Here and there, little puddles had begun steaming under the clear, bright sky. The townsfolk began watching the Silver Sliver. They waited anxiously for Mayor Selbie to retrieve the hunter and see what he was capable of. A little after noon, Grimluk stepped out on the porch and stood to wait under the shade of the awning.

A short while later, Mayor Selbie, Sadie, and two Watchmen came calling. The mayor was holding a small box, the Watchmen following him, pushing a cart with a large crate on it. Selbie smiled as Grimluk approached.

"Hello again. Ready to go?"

"Yes, let's get this over with," Grimluk said with a hint of his frustration.

"Good, good. Let's get things moving then."

Selbie led the group out of town. He nodded politely at Trilgor and the two Watchmen at the gate. Several yards away, he stopped the procession and waited a moment, letting the townsfolk who'd begun trickling out gather to watch. When he was satisfied, he opened his little box and pulled out a round, white amulet with a dark gem in its center. Selbie tucked the box under his armpit before slipping the cord over his head. The Watchmen removed the crate from the cart and left.

"Thank you, Grimluk," Selbie shouted, so the crowd could hear. "We appreciate your humor in this matter. Ladies and gentleman," he turned to face the town, "let the test begin!" He turned to the crate and gave it a solid kick, causing something inside to rattle loudly. As Mayor Selbie looked at Grimluk, the amulet flashed for a brief moment. "I'd just like to say, I'm sorry in advance if this doesn't end well for you." He gave the crate another kick, frowning as he did so. "Get up, already," he said flatly.

The contents rattled again, heavier this time. Something that sounded like dry-heaving came from inside it and before Grimluk could ask what was going on, the crate's lid burst open with a slam, breaking the clasp that had held it closed, splintering the wood. A gloved hand rested in the air where it had hit the lid. A second later, the hand fell, grabbing the side of the crate. Another hand joined it, pulling their owner up to a sitting position.

Grimluk could feel the eyes on him, staring out from behind stringy, dull hair. A figure in black climbed to its feet, stepping out of the crate, a heavy-booted foot stomping into the dirt. The figure began dry-heaving again, louder now that it was standing in the open. Its coat and clothes were covered in dirt, pebbles of debris rolling from the thing's crushed hat. Selbie walked up to stand next to it.

Grimluk's lips curled into a snarl. The man before him, once a pale elf, glared from a rotting shell, most of his flesh taut and decayed but appeared to be filling with life once more. Bones, both broken and whole, poked out of some places where worms and beetles had been feasting. The dead elf's eyes shown as vividly as they had in life, though now tarnished by rage and hatred. Grimluk was thankful the corpse wasn't fresh as the stink of death wafted towards his nose, assaulting it.

"A ghoul?" Grimluk asked.

"Ald'n," Selbie called, ignoring the hunter's question. The ghoul turned to him and growled.

"Thech-" More of the dry-heaving sound followed the elf's attempt to speak. He hacked and choked before hurling a wad of black phlegm from his throat. "Thhhhe *fuck*...do you want...old man?" The voice that issued forth from the dead elf's mouth sounded like gravel scraping flesh. "Why...am I...alive again?"

"It's very simple," the mayor said as he stepped in front of the elf. "You failed to help this town and now you're going to make up for it. You're going to do your best to kill the orc behind me."

Grimluk looked on in surprise, having never seen a talking ghoul before.

"And what...if I...kill you...instead?" Ald'n threatened Selbie.

"Oh, you're free to try but you're very much a dog on a short leash, so you'll be doing this thing for me whether you want to or not. And I don't honestly care what you want."

Ald'n snarled, swinging a tattered arm at the mayor's head with the same force that had blown the crate's lid off. It did not connect. His arm hung in the air, the decayed fist shaking several inches from the old man's face.

The mayor smiled. "I hope you feel better. Now, if you don't mind, I'm going to step back and you're going to try to kill the hunter. Do I make myself clear?" Ald'n's arm fell back to his side. He made no visible reply. Selbie smirked as he stepped briskly away from the would-be adversaries.

Grimluk moved without warning. His fist slammed into the elf's head like a boulder, backed by the full force of his weight. The sound of a thick, crunchy snap echoed before being swallowed by a great gasp from their audience. Ald'n's head had snapped back completely and dangled from a strand of nerves and flesh. The sound made Selbie turn round while the townsfolk let out a collective gasp of surprise. Grimluk shook his fist out and looked at the mayor.

"That it?"

"My boy, you're hardly done yet," the mayor replied, continuing to walk away.

Grimluk returned his gaze to the still standing body. It swayed drunkenly for a moment before reaching back and grabbing its dangling head. Grimluk watched as it pulled its head back into a vertical position. The muscle and bone began knitting itself back together. Ald'n let go of his head and glared at the orc. Grimluk saw then that the elf's whole body was repairing itself. Holes mended, bones reset, and rot disappeared. He wondered if the thing before him was actually a ghoul.

Grimluk took the sight of his test in. Reaching behind his back, he unsheathed the huge knife he wore, readying himself to slam it down into his enemy's head. His arm rose, tensing up like the bending shaft of a catapult before slamming down an instant later. The blade blasted through the top of the ghoul's skull up to the guard. The impact brought the creature to its knees.

"That was good," Ald'n growled. He reached up with a newly whole hand and pulled the blade out. A thick, black liquid squirted out with it. "Now it's my turn."

Ald'n struck out like a viper and headbutted Grimluk square in the chest hard enough to push him back a step. The elf struck again with a quick flurry of blows; a left jab to Grimluk's jaw, a hard right to his gut, and a spinning backhand that led Ald'n into a further spin, using his momentum to take Grimluk down with a sweep of the legs. Grimluk left the earth for a moment before landing hard on his back, knocking the air out of him.

Grimluk barely had time to catch his breath before Ald'n was on him again. The dead man was quick but not quick enough. Grimluk's hand shot up, grabbing the elf's wrist ferociously, and twisted it back with a sick snap. The knife flew from the elf's hand. Grimluk's grip remained tight. The elf growled and began throwing punches with his left arm. At point blank range, he couldn't miss. Grimluk didn't let go. He knocked Ald'n's arm away grabbed the elf's throat and hurled him away, quickly climbing to his feet. A moment later, Ald'n was on him again. Grimluk's fist exploded into the elf's stomach with such force that it lifted the lithe frame off the ground briefly. Ald'n hardly flinched at the attack but staggered back all the same. Grimluk stepped in quickly and slammed his entire arm into the ghoul's chest. As they fell, the orc drove his elbow down into Ald'n's chest. Bones snapped on impact as the elf's rib cage almost shattered.

Grimluk rolled away and got back to his feet. A wad of spit and blood landed a few feet away with a wet splat. Ald'n got to his feet slowly as his rib cage knit itself back together. Hatred beamed out from his eyes like two fury-filled stars. The two stared each other down. The wind kicked up tiny dust devils around them. Silence drew itself up close and gripped all who could see the two waging their battle.

"At this rate, we'll be at this all day, orc."

"You got a better idea, ghoul?"

Ald'n grinned and pulled back the right side of his coat, revealing a dirty pistol holstered to his thigh. "We draw." He unfastened the leather strip that had kept the pistol in place up until now.

Grimluk did the same and watched his opponent with all his focus. Muscles tensed and relaxed, winding up, ready to snap at the right moment. Ald'n once again displayed his speed. In the blink of an eye, he pulled his piece and slapped the hammer. Grimluk let out a grunt. The bullet had slammed into the right side of his chest. Two more shots rang out. A new hole opened up on the left side of his chest, and another above the first shot.

Grimluk remained on his feet, pulling out his own revolver. There was no quick-draw, only a deliberate aiming at his adversary. Another shot rang out from the elf's gun, hitting him in the center of his chest. He rocked slightly, but took aim, cocked the hammer, and pulled the trigger. The shot rang out like a cannon. The bullet ripped through Ald'n's torso and exploded through his back, taking a chunk of viscera and spine with it. Ald'n's legs went rubbery and then he collapsed.

Grimluk holstered his revolver as he walked over to his fallen foe. Ald'n still twitched, his face a mask of ferocity. He started to raise his gun only to have it kicked away. Grimluk watched as the elf's body again started pulling itself back together, albeit much slower this time. He brought a heavy boot down onto the elf's head, crushing it.

"Is this how it'll go? Will we keep fighting until he kills me or I collapse from destroying him?" he asked, turning his head to Mayor Selbie.

"You haven't stopped him yet. That's the test."

"The only thing that's been tested is my patience, old man. You control him. Stop this and let him stay dead or I will rip you in half and leave you for the vultures." Ald'n dug his fingers into Grimluk's leg but didn't have the power to push it away. The hunter's foot remained rooted in place like a centuries old oak tree, as he stared Selbie down hard.

The old man began to fidget. Ald'n's fingers dug in deeper, looking to pierce flesh and dig out the very muscles holding him at bay. Selbie finally sighed. "That's enough, you miserable piece of trash," he spat.

The amulet flashed again. Ald'n's fingers went slack and fell away from Grimluk's leg, the elf's body going silent and cold again. Grimluk looked down at the corpse and sneered. He scanned the area for his knife, catching sight of the glinting blade, half-covered in the dirt and retrieved it. He wiped the dust and black fluid covering the blade off on the bottom of his coat before slipping it behind his back again. His gaze worked back towards Selbie once more. He walked over to the little man and bent down, eye to eye, and spoke quietly. "If you do not bury that man properly, I will make things very unpleasant for you."

Mayor Selbie refused to look Grimluk in the eye, attempting to avoid Grimluk's gaze by looking at his chest. Blood leaked out of the bullet wounds. Then Selbie's eyes fell to the necklace around Grimluk's neck. Leather cord ran through the center of nine lead slugs. In surprise, he looked up at Grimluk and gulped. Fear of the hunter invaded his heart. He nodded meekly.

"Good. Do it now and while you're at it, send Sadie to see me at the Silver Sliver." Grimluk turned and head back into town. The townsfolk parted for him, unsure whether to fear him or celebrate the possibility of a savior. Mayor Selbie followed shortly, moving slowly like a scolded dog.

"Are you okay? What did he say?" Sadie asked her boss.

"Mind your own goddamn business," he snapped, baring his teeth for a moment. "The hunter wants to talk to you. Don't-" but he stopped.

Grimluk lumbered back up the stairs of the Silver Sliver towards his room. He pushed the door open slowly and slipped inside, leaving it cracked slightly for Sadie. His coat and hat found their previous resting places on the back of the chair near the window, this time carelessly. The gun belt dropped to the floor next to the chair with a heavy thud. His shirt dropped to the floor as well, rolling out of his left hand as he sank into the free chair and leaned his head back against the wall. A minute or so later, he heard a small knock on the door.

"Enter," he rumbled.

The door slid open and quietly shut again as Sadie entered. She stood in awkward silence, staring at Grimluk's bleeding chest, watching it move with slow, deliberate breaths.

"I'm grateful you agreed to come," he said, looking down at the small woman. He reached into his bag and pulled out a roll of leather. "And I'd like to say I'm sorry we ruined your soufflé."

Sadie laughed, surprising herself, but venting some of her anxiety.

Grimluk spread the roll out on the table. An array of items clinked, each housed in a pocket and tied down with a thin strip. Needles, thread, a strange device with a claw at its end, bandages, and a couple of small bottles of pale, thick salve.

"You're still a jackass," she said quietly and sternly, "but he was an asshole to test you like that. He says he has the town's best interest at heart but...I just...there had to have been a better way. And without digging up Ald'n." She trailed off.

Grimluk looked at her in stern contemplation. For a moment, he debated asking if Selbie really *did* have the town's best interest at heart but shots of pain rain through his chest, recalling his attention. "Not to sound selfish but my chest is holding half a chamber of lead and I'd like to get it out. It's startin' to itch."

"What do you want me to do?" Sadie asked

Grimluk motioned for Sadie to step forward while he stretched out his foot and pulled the chair holding his coat and hat over in front of him. He reached over and plucked the strange claw device from its resting spot. "This is a slug-puller," he said, holding it up. "Normally, I do this myself but it's much easier to have someone else do it. You'll slide it into the wound, move the little trigger and grab the lead. Then pull. Hard or slow, whichever you feel comfortable doing."

Sadie blanched. "You want me to what?!" She looked at him in utter disbelief.

Grimluk sighed. "It's not as bad as it sounds. And I need them out." He held out the little contraption. Sadie took it, looking at it like it was threatening her. Grimluk grabbed the underside of the chair, baring his chest and rooting himself. Sadie swallowed, her mouth suddenly dry, steadying herself as best she could before moving her hand forward towards the wound on the left first.

Grimluk barely flinched as Sadie dug the first slug out of his chest. He felt a moment of pressure as she pressed the extractor's tip into the lead, and then relief as she pulled it out. He held out his hand and she dropped the slug into it. They breathed out in unison. Grimluk set himself once more. Sadie held her breath and went in again. He winced this time, just for a second, the central wound next to his breastbone.

"That one'll hurt for a while," Grimluk remarked rather casually. He felt another moment of pressure and then more relief. Sadie held the bullet over his open hand, releasing it to join its sibling. She steadied herself again with another deep breath for the third bullet.

"Did he say anything to you?" Grimluk asked her. Pressure, relief.

"No," Sadie finally answered, readying to finish

the last wound. "But he doesn't usually. He...tolerates my occasional attitude because I do my job well, but he doesn't particularly like me. I don't know that he actually likes anyone though. He can seem friendly enough at times but I wonder. And he's one of a few who've been here since the town's early days."

Grimluk felt one final push of pressure before Sadie pulled the last slug free along with a small spurt of blood. Sadie grabbed a bandage and pressed it down quickly as he took the slug-puller and the last slug away. The other wounds barely bled in comparison but she packed the bandage on tight and held it there with a surprising amount of force.

"He resurrected a dead hunter with some powerful magic and seemed pretty intent on the elf killing me," Grimluk remarked while she staunched the wound.

Sadie frowned, staring hard at nothing in particular. Her mind was a jumble.

"Can you help me with talking to the townsfolk?" Grimluk asked.

"I suppose," she said with a touch of confusion. "Why would you need my help though? I don't know what I'm doing."

Grimluk grabbed the needle and thread, setting to work stitching himself up, almost absentmindedly. His hands moved with smoothness that said he'd done this before. "I need an advocate. Right now, no one knows whether to fear me or help me. You're one of them and they'd probably feel more at ease with a familiar face. Familiarity tends to keep folks calmer. I'm willing to pay, of course. Ten bilts."

Sadie's eyes went wide and she stared at him, trying to make sure he was serious. "Ten bilts is a lot of money," she said, still watching him. He just nodded. "Alright," she said apprehensively.

"We can give everyone a couple of days to settle. I'll go talk to Trilgor too. He can have a Watchman relay any plans we make. I want to make sure everyone can prepare in whatever way they see fit."

Grimluk finished sewing himself up. He grabbed the roll of bandages and a bottle of salve. The salve plopped out of its bottle and onto the bandage, adhering the bandages to his flesh like a healing glue. He pressed each strip down hard, turning the green flesh of his chest and fingertips pale for a moment. The strips held fast.

"And Sadie, if you're willing, I need you to tell me if anything strange occurs with Mayor Selbie. Could just be your little infestation has hit him hard. But if not..."

"Yeah," she sighed, "yeah, I'll try to let you know if I see anything." She hoped this would pay off in the end and not come back to bite her in the ass. "Besides, I wanna know too."

That night, Kenton Selbie sat behind his desk, staring into the flickering darkness of his office. He was alone, save for a bottle of whiskey and a lone kerosene lamp sitting at the corner of the desk. The small flame's light washed over his face, danced in bleary and bloodshot eyes. He'd dismissed Sadie as soon as she returned and fell into the bottle right away. She'd have a mess to clean up when she arrived the next day.

He started. He'd heard something. Something that sounded far away. Something getting closer.

Something mocking him.

Cruel laughter filled the dark as it pushed out the dim light from the lamp. The shadows wrapped around the old man's desk. The laughter circled Selbie, causing the shadows to pulsate around him. Had he been sober, the effect still would've made him dizzy but being drunk off of his ass, he nearly vomited.

The laughter turned to words. "Poor little Selbie, so upset about the orc." The words came from nowhere and everywhere. "Poooooor little Selbiii-ieeee." The shadows swirled out in front of Selbie's desk. He looked away as the shadows took shape. The form mocked the limitations of mortal flesh, unwilling to stay concise and complete. It casually climbed upon the desk and sat cross-legged. One, huge, glowing yellow eye opened slowly, staring down at him. "Your orc problem should be fun to watch."

"Fucker rolls into town and...and..."

"And what?" it spat back at him.

And what, indeed, Selbie thought. And he survived. And he sees through me. And he makes me afraid. "And thinks he's some fucking hero. Thinks he knows what's best for this town. *I* know what's best," Selbie blustered loudly, hoping the focus on the town would eradicate his fear.

The shadow creature laughed once more. The light from the lamp dimmed in time with the laughter. "Oh, Selbie, don't think I can't see it. You're afraid of him. I saw it clearly, so *very* clearly. He reached into your black little heart and squeezed it until your veins iced over. Are you not better than some filthy orc? Are you not smarter than him? Why should you fear such a creature as this Grimluk?" Every syllable dripped with derision.

Selbie stewed, refusing to look at the chiding mockery of a face. He would have to let the orc do his work for now. The whiskey bottle met his lips once more, rolling down his throat in a burning wave. "What do you want me to do?" Selbie asked the thing on his desk.

"I want you to wait for now. Your little failure of a test doesn't change anything. You will wait, I will watch. The orc is no threat to me. I existed when his people were still savage beasts and I'll exist long after you all." The shadows leaned towards Selbie's face, forcing him to look into the glowing eye and swirling shadows.

Selbie's head swam, making him shut his eyes hard. A few moments later, through silence and the weight of the demon's presence now lifted from him, he knew he was alone again. He sighed and rubbed his eyes before capping the bottle of whiskey and wandering off to find his bed.

CHAPTER 4

When Grimluk awoke the next morning, the salve had worked its healing magic and knit the bullet holes in his chest closed. The wounds ached dully but only from the stiffness of the rejuvenated flesh. He rubbed each spot gently until the aches had quieted down. By nightfall, he'd be able to remove the bandages. Faded scars would remain, new mementos added to his collection from fights past. Grimluk gathered his hat and gun belt, opting to leave his coat where it was, folded over a chair. He slung his bag over his shoulders and departed his room.

Mattias's ever friendly face greeted him from his post behind the bar. Grimluk ordered breakfast and ate in silence. The Silver Sliver remained mostly empty, as it had since he'd arrived. A few people had wandered in the previous night, mostly to see if they could catch a glimpse of the hunter. He'd motioned for them to join him. They did not accept the invitation and instead hastily turned away. They were gone after a pint each. He hoped, over his eggs and sausage, that Trilgor and Sadie could help him earn the town's trust.

A short while later, he said as much to the young captain. Grimluk explained his plan as he had to

Sadie. Trilgor agreed to it. He called over a Watchman, a young man with wheat-colored hair. Trilgor informed the young man what he would be doing as he scribbled down the proper information for his charge. He handed over the page and sent the young man out.

"Quite the show yesterday," Trilgor remarked after a moment of silence.

Grimluk grunted. "Hope so. Took four slugs to put it on."

Trilgor shook his head. "You looked like a tough cuss but four shots to the chest and I'm still amazed you're standing here."

"All that talk about your mother and you sure do impress easily," Grimluk teased. He absently rubbed his chest as he grinned. "Way you tell it, she could have kicked my ass up and down the Wastelands."

Trilgor let out a chuckle that turned into a full-bellied laugh. "She'd have told ya the same too!"

"So, I got a few days to prepare for interviews. Anything I should know? Any morsels of advice for an ol' demon-puncher?"

Trilgor let out a solitary laugh at that. "Not as such but I do have someone you might want to talk to." Grimluk raised an eyebrow. "Elf we got locked up still. First..." He hesitated. "I hate to call him a murderer. He was a good person before that night in the mine. Still is...or would be. His mind's all but gone now. He just babbles about that night over and over again."

A rumble from Grimluk's throat. "Mm, first one to succumb, then?"

"I'd guess so. First person to have a violent

episode anyway."

"Think he'd be up for a chat?"

"I'd bet so. Might have to break it up if he gets excited though."

Grimluk held his arm out. "Lead the way."

Trilgor took led him towards the other side of the building where the cells sat. There were four, each wall and door made of iron bars. Each cell was big enough to house someone of Grimluk's size but only if they stayed still. At the end of the hallway, in the last cell, sat a scraggly-haired elf, curled up in a ball on the cot.

"Negos," Trilgor called. Not even a twitch. "Got a visitor for you. Wants to hear your story."

The elf tensed. He turned worn eyes towards the pair. "Who?"

"My name is Grimluk. I'm a demon hunter."

Negos covered his head and started shouting. "No! I didn't mean to! I'm not a demon!"

Grimluk waited for him to calm some. "It's okay, I know you're not a demon. I want to hear what happened to you. That's all."

Negos fell silent. Slowly, he sat up, facing the orcs. Some semblance of lucidity appeared on his face. "Alright...my story...okay..." His voice sounded far away. "I didn't mean to do it, ya see. It just happened."

****

Negos and Franklin began their night like most. As the day shift cleared out, they, along with the other night crew, headed down into the mine to expand existing tunnels or clear out new ones for further extraction. Tonight would be a simple expansion for the pair. The elf and human had worked with each other for years and while they found they didn't have a whole lot in common, they enjoyed each other's company all the same. Franklin had once pointed out that they shared enough of a similar sense of humor that it kept their hours underground fairly smooth.

The two miners, dressed in thick denim coveralls and strong, steel-toed boots, strapped on their tool belts and requisitioned some small explosives from their foreman, a dwarf by the name of Orn Shatter-stone. Orn sported a close-cut head of hair along with one of the signatures of his people, a prodigious beard. Both were gray with age. The other signature of his people was present as well, as he only stood about even with most of the other miners' chests. He was a demolitions expert and older than most of them. He was occasionally gruff, as some of the younger guys found out from a black eye, but he was mostly affable.

With explosives and tools gathered, the two made their way down the main shaft. Of the four tunnels, they were working on the back left. The silver vein in that shaft was still good but was starting to get cramped at the end. Negos, with his stronger eyes, examined the back wall and marked off four spots with chalk.

"These should work for the sticks," he said to Franklin.

"Alright, then," Franklin nodded and pulled his hand-drill from his belt. "Let's get this fucker down then."

Negos pulled a dirty, brown bandanna from his

pocket and tied around his forehead. He did this more to keep the shaggy mop of dirty-blond hair out of his eyes than for sweat. His compatriot's dark hair stayed cropped close enough he never much felt the need for anything other than his sleeve for sweat. Franklin had teased him once about the bandanna.

"Wouldn't want to stain those blue eyes with a little sweat, would ya, buddy?"

Negos had rolled his eyes at this and always did so when Franklin still occasionally brought the crack up again.

They got right to work, cranking their drills solidly until four neat little holes formed, big enough for their explosives to slide into. In the sticks went. Their long fuses dangled out before being lit. The two men stepped back a few feet and turned away. A moment later, the rock wall exploded. As Negos turned toward the dust cloud, he jumped and gasped.

"What?!" Franklin shouted with a start.

"I...fuck. Fuckin' smoke. Thought I saw somethin'." Negos stared into the haze.

"Gods damn, you 'bout made my heart bust through my chest," Franklin said, taking a deep breath.

The pair sighed and laughed it off. Smoke and dull light can play with your eyes sometimes, they told themselves. The real surprise was an elf seeing something that wasn't there. Negos knew his friend would rib him about it and sure enough, after they'd both calmed down, Franklin said it.

"Guess them blues a yours finally got dirty, eh?"

"Yeah, yeah," Negos said shaking his head. "Still better than them mud balls you got, I reckon."

They continued their work for another hour uninterrupted before Franklin saw something. As they were clearing away the rubble, dumping it in the tunnel's cart, Franklin startled at what he swore was a "big fuckin worm" wriggling from out of the tunnel wall. Negos insisted it was just a trick of light, just like before. Franklin rubbed his jaw in thought before reluctantly agreeing. It hadn't felt like a trick of light but then, he reasoned, did tricks ever feel like tricks?

Over the next few hours, Franklin kept seeing his worm and each time, it seemed to get a little more agitated. The worm, white as bone and as big as Franklin's forearm, would slowly creep out from the rock and then start writhing violently at him. He swore it was like it was trying to get out and land on him, that the thing had teeth.

Negos would see Franklin's face suddenly appear too close, except it wasn't quite his friend's face. It was off. Sometimes, he'd catch the eyes just long enough to see they were faintly glowing red. Sometimes, he wouldn't even register it until it smiled at him and rotten, yellow teeth, jagged and misshapen, would catch his eye. At one point, he turned to catch sight of the phantom only to see Franklin staring at him.

Things proved no better after an early lunch break and some fresh air. They stood in the faint moonlight outside of the front building of the mine where the office and miners' housing was located. They did their best to brush things off. Just nerves and making one another jumpy. The meal and air helped put their minds back at ease before returning to the tunnel. Even with their reasoning and slight revitalization, the apparitions returned. Franklin cussed at the worm thing before he went to get an extra lamp to keep at their feet. He figured the extra light would help. At the least, he pointed out, it couldn't hurt. The extra light did seem to help as neither one of them saw anything further.

After a while, however, Negos stopped again and turned to Franklin. "The fuck are you mumbling about?"

"The fuck are you on about?" Franklin replied, looking confused.

"I'm over here working in silence and you keep mumbling. Shut the fuck up, okay?"

Franklin glowered at Negos. "Your ears have gone to shit now too," he grumbled.

The pair attempted to return to working in silence again. The only sound that of their picks and hammers wearing down ancient stone. The silence could not last though. Franklin would occasionally look over at Negos to see how he was doing. Negos's ears kept twitching every time Franklin would look at him. Franklin would return to his work but it didn't seem to matter. Negos kept getting more tense and disturbed. Each time Franklin looked over at him, Negos's shoulders grew tighter. The rhythm of his pick grew slower.

Franklin finally stopped work altogether and turned to his friend, his own body and mind growing more tense from the affair. "You alright, Negos?"

A start ran across the miner's back. He stopped working and stood up in silence. Franklin shifted uneasily. The air hung still as death save for the sound of Negos's breathing and the faint noise of the other night crews working. Franklin began to ask again but was cut off.

"Stop looking at me like that." The tone was cold as ice and just as stiff.

"Yeah, okay, how bout we get some more air again? Or you can go alone, I won't look at ya." Franklin rubbed his jaw idly after speaking, spreading dust as he did so.

"I'll get air when I fucking feel like it, you just turn your ass around and stop looking at me. And keep your mouth shut while you do it. Only thing I wanna hear from you is steel against rock, you understand me?"

"Yeah," Franklin said, turning back around, "just calm down."

Quiet descended once more upon the miners and their work. Franklin tried to work quieter, even breathe quieter, but it didn't seem to be working. Negos, frustration growing, kept thinking he was seeing Franklin looking at him again. Bastard was doing it to spite him, he thought, and moving too fast to get caught. He whirled on his partner. "I told ya to stop that, you stupid pile of shit!"

"Negos, I ain't been doing nothing but smashin' rocks! You're the one makin' all the noise now. How 'bout *you* shut the fuck up and get back to work? You fucking understand *that*?"

The two glared at each other, their faces covered in rock dust, their eyes bloodshot from the same, and the growing tension. Negos, with his intense blue eyes, looked like a man possessed. He was the first to break eye contact. He turned back around and faced the rock once more. He realized after a moment that his hand hurt. He looked down at it. His knuckles were bloodless and pale as he squeezed the handle of his pick.

He loosened his grip and then tightened it again. He suddenly imagined the handle as Franklin's throat and smiled. That let him get back to work. He felt some of his tension relieved as he began picking away once more at the rock. Until he heard Franklin cough.

The scream echoed through the tunnels. It hit every ear louder than it had any right to be. The sound drowned out any sound that should've overpowered it. All the miners converged in the main chamber, save for two. Orn took a head count to confirm, not that he needed to. The old dwarf took off for the back tunnel, the others following him. They murmured to themselves, wondering if the missing pair had been hurt or trapped. And if trapped, how in the gods' names did no one feel the quaking of the tunnel collapsing?

Negos stood over Franklin's body with a hammer in his hand. His pickax stood up out from his former partner's back. The hammer dripped with blood and brain. Negos's body shook as he sucked in labored breaths.

"Negos," Orn half-shouted.

Negos turned his head slowly towards his peers. His face was covered in Franklin's blood. His eyes were wide and staring, covered in strange shadows from the fallen lamp Franklin had retrieved previously. As Negos registered his coworkers' presence, the hammer fell from his hand, clattering on the stone, the wooden handle landing in a puddle of blood with a wet slap. He looked around for a second like he had just been roused from a deep dream.

"What-" he started to say before looking down at Franklin's corpse. Blood was still pooling under the body in a thick puddle, but worse yet was the crushed mess where the man's head had once been. Negos retched. Everyone looked on in stunned silence.

"What happened?" he implored more than asked. "What the fuck happened? What happened?!"

He kept repeating the question but he knew the answer. He sank to his knees and clutched his face. Orn turned his head to the woman behind him, telling her to go get the Watch. She backed out slowly and did as she was asked. Negos was screaming again by the time she got out of the mine. The sound haunted her. Haunted them all.

Negos stood unsteadily and took a lumbering step towards Orn. The old dwarf's body tensed up, ready to respond if attacked. Tears streaked down the elf's face, mingling with Franklin's blood, rock dust, and his own sweat. His body shook with great sobs. Negos had never even been in a fist fight before and here he was, covered in his friend's blood.

"What did I do?" he croaked through a sob.

Orn and the rest of the night shift remained silent and unsure. Each shuffled uncomfortably and whispered to each other. One of the miners, an elf man with dark skin, pale yellow eyes, and a loose ponytail inched close to Orn's shoulder.

"What do we do, Orn?"

"Only thing we can do," he whispered back, "make sure he doesn't get away until the Watch gets here." Orn realized a moment later he should have just ignored the elf. Negos heard "the Watch" and snapped back to his feet ready to belt anyone who got near him. He said as much as well. Orn put his hands up to show he meant no threat to the maddened elf but Negos was gone again, back into his mutterings, eyes filled with anger. He charged the old dwarf.

A short time later, the woman Orn sent off returned with three Watchmen following her. Each member, a human man and woman, and a dwarf man, carried a revolver and a club at their side. The woman was the tallest and led the posse. When they arrived at the scene, Orn and two other miners had pinned Negos down. He attempted to thrash about but the trio had him down tight, pinning his limbs. They wanted to keep him from attacking anyone, not kill him.

"I'd be real grateful if y'all could get him chained up and out of here before something else happens," Orn said as the three Watchmen came into his view.

The Watchmen snapped into motion, as both of the men slapped shackles onto Negos's wrists and ankles. The miners attempted to help get Negos up to his feet again but the elf headbutted Orn. Instead of walking him out after that, the Watchmen lifted him up by his arms and feet, carrying him back to the jail as best they could without hurting him or being hurt themselves. As they exited the mine and walked across town to the jail, the sun began to creep up. The pale dawn light grew steadily, rising on the first murder Greenreach Bluffs had had in decades.

****

73

After listening to Negos's story, and thanking Trilgor, Grimluk returned to his room to meditate on the details. It was more than clear that the elf's mind had deteriorated mostly from the shock of murdering his friend, but the speed at which his mind had been seized was frightening. Though it stood to reason that the demon's influence could have built up slowly over time and finally boiled over.

It was more information though. He would get more details from the other denizens of the town about what was happening, but for now, he had Thomas's story as well and that was a good start for a town that hadn't wanted his help at first. After lunch, he would visit the magician.

CHAPTER 5

Grimluk thought about visiting the blacksmith first. He could see the man sitting behind his anvil in an old rocker, arms crossed, and a look on his face that dared Grimluk to try and speak to him. Instead, he just nodded at the smith and moved. That was good enough for now. He would speak to the man in time.

As Grimluk approached the general store, he noticed a young boy, about eleven or twelve years old sitting on the porch, brown eyed with dark, shaggy hair. He sat quietly, his legs dangling in faded denim just above the dirt. Grimluk greeted him, but the boy made no reply, continuing to watch him with vague curiosity. Behind the boy, peeking into the shop's window, was a little girl similarly dark hair, about six or seven, in a little brown dress. She heard Grimluk's greeting and turned, gasping at the sight of him the way only little children do.

She smiled and waved at him. "Hi, Mr. Orc," she blurted cheerfully.

"Hello, little one," Grimluk replied, returning the smile. The boy continued watching in silence. "How are you?"

"Good," she said, holding the word out. The door to the store opened and the girl turned around.

A woman with mouse-brown hair stepped out, holding a basket. "Momma!" she shouted and hugged her mother's leg.

The woman stopped, locking eyes with him. A small frown came to her lips but when she looked down at her daughter's big smile, it faded. "Are you two ready?" she asked.

"Can I say bye to Mr. Orc first?" the girl asked.

"Okay, Gwenny. Nicholas, are you ready?"

"Yes, Momma." He stood, still watching Grimluk.

Gwen leaped off the porch, out in front of him before turning to him and raising her hand into the air. "Bye, Mr. Orc!"

"Goodbye, little one." He looked at her mother as she stepped down. "Ma'am," he said, touching the brim of his hat. He watched as the three left. The store's owner, an elf, stood at the door, watching him. Her face was untrusting, her mouth drawn into a thin slit. Her eyes were just as shrewd as Mattias's.

Grimluk greeted the woman, touching the brim of his hat. "Ma'am." She replied with a curt nod before stepping back into her shop slamming the door behind her. "I hope the magician's friendlier than this," Grimluk muttered to himself.

The afternoon sun crept lazily across the sky, still high and strong as Grimluk started making his way towards the strange building in the back corner of the town. The wood structure he had glimpsed days prior was actually a formal entryway. Pillars of wood held a steep roof aloft. The walkway itself was smooth stone, cobbled together in various shades and tones, brought from the mine. Along the walkway were long planters filled with ferns and small flowers. The planters were painted in light colors. The mouth of the temple was a carved opening in the bluff behind the back town wall. It was much simpler in comparison to the wood entryway, mostly being a large, rectangular opening.

Grimluk made his way in. The way was lit only by outside light for a time before opening into a large cavern. The walls were covered in sconces with torches, most lit, while other spots had hooks with lanterns hanging on them. He was almost surprised to see that this place was not a place of worship. It was more like a clinic in some respects. One area housed cots and what looked like a table covered in first aid supplies. Chairs and small tables were littered about, like the place sometimes served for small social gatherings. Several other openings led farther back into the cave, with one still being lit.

"I seek the magician that dwells here," Grimluk said. His voice bounced off the cave, echoing. He waited a moment but no response. He decided to move towards the lit tunnel.

It was a short walk, leading to a small room. In it sat a desk, a bookcase, and a bed. On the bed lay a portly man. His hair was long, tied back, and nearly white. Grimluk grimaced in surprise at seeing the man was naked save for a loincloth. He attempted to rouse the man by clearing his throat loudly. The magician rolled over away from the orc. Grimluk tried again. No response.

"Wake up, old man," he finally shouted.

The magician turned violently then and hurled the pillow at Grimluk's face with surprising speed. "Fuck off!"

Grimluk held the pillow, literally dumbstruck. The old man curled back up, ignoring him. He sneered and hurled the pillow back at its owner. "Old man, get up right now or I will get you up myself," he said, his voice rumbling in agitation.

"What time is it?" the old man grumbled without moving.

"After noon."

"...this better be an emergency," the old man said as he rolled over, finally laying eyes on the one disturbing his sleep. "Oh...it's you. I guess that means this mostly *is* an emergency. Alright, alright. Go back out and I'll be there in a few minutes."

Grimluk grunted, eyeing the old man critically before turning back towards the main chamber again. After more than a few minutes, with Grimluk starting to lose his patience, the old magician appeared from his little room, fully dressed now in a ratty old robe. His eyes were bright, or would have been if it weren't for the glaze of sleep still sitting in them. The magician walked past Grimluk making for one of the tables and its two chairs. The hunter followed, watching the old man collapse into his chair with a dull thump. Grimluk sat lightly down onto the other chair. The wood let out a soft groan.

"So, mister, uh...Grimelan, wasn't it?" Grimluk corrected him. "Ah, pardon. Now that you've woke me, what can the great and powerful Ivor Danshor do for you?" He yawned.

"A great and powerful magician who snores the day away?" The shadow of sarcasm covering Grimluk's words.

"Magicians aren't allowed to sleep late?"

"You run a temple. Most holy men are a touch more punctual in my experience."

The magician laughed. It was loud and deep and echoed a long time after it ended. "Holy-HA! Holy man, oh, hunter, I see you're here to murder me with laughter. I'm not holy. 'Holy' is a myth. No, I'm just a magician. And an old one at that." Ivor wiped away a stray tear as he spoke. His body shook with small aftershocks of amusement as one arm came to rest on top of his belly as he regarded Grimluk with amusement.

"I see. Then I will ask my first question of you."

"Yes?"

Grimluk's nearly black eyes locked onto the magician's. He wore a look of both tenacity and intimidation. It strove to dive into the old man's con-science, to provoke him to speak truth. It was something he'd had to learn to do in his travels, espe-cially useful for those who were less than truthful. There were times when those with power had been behind the atrocities and problems he had witnessed or helped solve but they broke easily with the right look, whether by confessing or giving themselves away. "Did you summon the demon that plagues this town, old man?"

Ivor's face changed, the amusement replaced with a staggered bemusement. He held Grimluk's gaze, meeting it fully and showing himself plainly. "I see, I see. You've definitely got some sand in your craw. Hm, I'll tell you a little about me then. And don't look at me like that, I'll keep it relevant, explain why an old fart like me is out here. I'm not so old that my brain has melted and made me a doddering fool."

Grimluk nodded and remained silent.

"Now, given you're a demon hunter, you know about the Wastelands and probably the rumors about what the dwarves did. That was probably fifty years ago now. And I was here when it happened. I was a young apprentice and believe me, Grimluk, when I say that the shit that flew out from wherever the fuck it all came from was pure terror. Sure, there were creatures of all kinds and even more demons released to walk free, but it was all fear and hate given form to scuttle across the earth. You've seen it for yourself but it's all spread out now. Over the course of the first few days, all that shit spewed out in waves.

"All the little annoying things came first. Like those little dust devils and the tricksters that'll get ya lost. Each time something new came barreling out, the ground got a little drier, and a little deader, and the things got a bit bigger, and a bit meaner, like the Abyss itself was leaking out. Seemed to make, well, *everything* a little worse too. I assume you've had to deal with ghouls before. Those were pretty rare once but not so much these days."

"Had to go through a pack of ghouls and a very unnatural dust-storm to get here," Grimluk noted.

"That right? Damn." Ivor sighed. "Well, my master felt everything spewin' out of whatever foul place it spewed out from. He could feel it all and he knew we had to get some sort of protection up. He's the one that created the barrier. We didn't get it up in time to completely spare ourselves some affliction from the rollin' evil."

Ivor paused for a moment, lingering on the word "evil." His eyes fell, some side memory caught in his mind for a moment. "He got it up before the big things arrived though. Not that you could see 'em all real good. Some were covered by clouds of dust but you could see their shadows. Some were blurry, like you couldn't focus on them. Or maybe they were just too terrible for any of us to comprehend. Maybe our minds were doing us a favor..."

Ivor drifted off into quiet again. His eyes still down. Lost in the memories, trying to push foul images back down.

"Anyways, he died in an attack by some of the nastier critters years later. We were setting up the stones around town, made from the big one he made originally. They still weren't so spread out and when we took the barrier down, it was like a dinner bell. I took over and I've been here since. So, my demon-killing friend, given what I've seen and given what I've done, no, I didn't summon the demon." Ivor looked up, meeting Grimluk's eyes again. His face was deadly serious. Quiet blanketed them.

Grimluk continued to scan for any deceit. Finally, he nodded. "You were having nightmares long before this happened, weren't you?"

"Yes."

"So you stayed put."

"I make potions, tend to the sick and injured, and help the farmers keep us fed. And most importantly, I keep that goddamn barrier up. And it keeps that shit out."

"If I need your help with this, can I count on you? Potions, research?" Grimluk folded his arms across his chest as he leaned back in his chair.

"Grimluk," Ivor began, "if it means kicking the shit out of a demon, I'll be glad to lend a hand. Or a boot."

Grimluk nodded. Things were starting to look up. "So," he began, "that just leaves the next question. How's the demon effected you?"

"Truthfully? I'm not sure it has, least not like most folks that it *has*. I been havin' nightmares for fifty years, I think the worst thing this demon has done to me is make them more frequent."

"And yet you love to sleep," Grimluk observed.

"Well, I do need my beauty sleep," Ivor said with a grin. Grimluk's eyebrow raised. "I'm old, Grimluk. I get tired easily and I try to reserve my energy for when I'm needed. Nightmares are just part of the landscape of my mind at this point."

Grimluk grunted. "I know the feeling."

"I'll bet you do." Ivor perked up suddenly, "Say, if you're not needed elsewhere, maybe you could give me some news from outside the borderlands. We don't get much out here and I'm sure a lot's happened in the past few years. Think of it as a bit of prepayment for my help." He winked.

Grimluk shrugged and spent the next few hours telling Ivor things he'd seen and heard on his travels. Ivor was particularly interested in hearing about a new rail transportation system that used fire and water elementals to power huge tanks that pulled cars along behind it.

Chapter 6

Sadie arrived at the Silver Sliver to join Grimluk for breakfast looking like she hadn't slept. Her eyes were puffy and she yawned constantly. When questioned, she simply mumbled the word "nightmares." Mattias's sausage and eggs left something to be desired but he always made good coffee. Sadie held a fresh cup, steaming and black, and took a sip. She started to perk up, regaining enough zest to all but banish her persistent yawning. After a second cup, she felt ready to meet the town with the hunter. Grimluk rose, making his way outside. Sadie followed, Grimluk holding the door for her.

"So, who's first?" she inquired.

"How well do you know the smith?"

"Only passingly. Only spoken to him a couple times."

"What about the elf that owns the store?"

"Jhaan? We're friendly. I do frequent her store quite a bit."

Grimluk grunted. "I know everyone's less than eager to speak with me. We'll start with her. Hopefully your presence will ease her trepidations. Wesson will probably remain silent with or without you. I'd appreciate it if you spoke to Jhaan before I entered."

"I can do that," she affirmed, before making her way to the store.

Sadie's shadow stretched out behind her in the morning sun. For a moment, Grimluk swore it bent at an impossible angle. He looked up, hoping maybe it had just be a wisp of cloud passing in front of the sun. Clear as crystal. He frowned and walked slowly after Sadie, letting her have time enough to talk to Jhaan. She disappeared into the building.

"Jhaan," Sadie called out as she closed the shop door.

"Sadie?" The voice came from the back of the shop.

"It's me."

"I'll be up in just a moment."

Sadie took in a deep breath, steadying herself. She hoped Jhaan wouldn't be too cross with her. Jhaan appeared from the back coming to greet her customer. Sadie watched as her face knotted up instead.

"What's wrong?"

"The demon hunter is standing outside." Jhaan's fists clenched.

Sadie sighed. "Yeah, about him..."

"Don't tell me you're here for him!" Jhaan shouted.

Sadie winced at the shout. For a moment, she thought she heard Jhaan growl. "Weeeell...if you want to get specific, I'm here for the town." She half-laughed at herself. "He's here to help us, Jhaan. I believe him when he says that. And if you need to, you can put this on my tab." She gave Jhaan a friendly smile.

Jhaan groaned, her fist clenching again. She stared at Sadie, eyes like daggers. "Fine...just fucking fine. Get that dumb-ass in here and let's get this over with."

Sadie poked her head out of the door and waved for Grimluk to come in.

"I suppose you expect me to break down into a beautiful catharsis, praising the great demon hunter, here to save us," Jhaan spat as he closed the door.

"Never been one for hero worship, ma'am. Usually leads to folks shooting at me," Grimluk replied with a smile. Sadie giggled when she looked at Jhaan's reaction. The woman's jaw had dropped, while a confused smile tugged at her mouth through sheer surprise at his reply. "All I want is to help, ma'am. And to avoid being shot at again if possible."

Jhaan took a deep breath, amusement washing over her for a moment, and then a rush of weariness. She gave her face a quick rub, letting the breath escaped her lips, and with it, some small piece of anxiety.

"Alright," her tone now much more amiable, "I still don't wanna talk about it but alright, let's get it over with."

Grimluk moved closer to Sadie and Jhaan. "I understand. Just start at the beginning and go from there."

"I don't remember everything from the beginning, honestly. I just remember when I realized I was being affected. I'm afraid I won't be much help beyond that. I was...I." Jhaan closed her eyes before taking another deep breath. She crossed her arms tightly. "I almost killed a child."

She looked up at Grimluk, expecting contempt but he held no judgment in is face that she could see. The lack of shock surprised her.

"But you didn't," he said, prompting her to continue.

"No...no but damn it, I came so close. I just...knew he was stealing something. I got so angry. And then I was standing over him with a knife." She paused. Her gaze had fallen far away. "He didn't notice me at first. He turned back, maybe to see if I was still there, I don't know. I still can't shake the feeling that he was stealing from me, so it still feels like he only looked back to check to see if I was paying attention.

"But there I was now and his eyes were huge. I remember my jaw hurt from clenching it so hard and that snapped me out of it. The boy ran off when I dropped the knife. I locked the door and closed shop." She trembled for a moment before stepping close to Grimluk, her fists balled up. She took in measured breaths, fighting down the urge to attack the hunter. She wanted to scream at Sadie too. Jhaan bottled it as best she could and stared into the shadowy pools of Grimluk's eyes, her jaw tight. "And if I'm honest, I'm convinced you're going to rob me as well."

"Thank you," Grimluk said gently, giving her a solemn nod. "I just have one more question, a simple one, if that's alright." Jhaan nodded. "Do you remember which child it was?"

She stood quietly, trying to remember. "No...no, I don't. All I remember is how big his eyes were. Was it even a boy?" A light groan escaped her lips. "I can't remember."

"That's fine, thank you, Jhaan. I'm sorry I had to send Sadie in first. If you can, maybe try to get a little sleep."

Jhaan let out a bitter laugh at the mention of sleep as Grimluk slipped away quietly. Sadie turned to Jhaan and gently touched her forearm. The two weren't exactly close but she still wanted to show the woman compassion. Jhaan started at the touch but didn't recoil. Sadie turned and joined Grimluk outside.

The pair stepped off the porch and turned left to round the store. Grimluk took his first good look at the housing arrangement for most of the town. The housing consisted of apartments built mostly from stone and crude masonry. The buildings lined the inner wall, facing toward the center of town. There was enough room behind them to line with a few outhouses. This particular building had been built for families.

There weren't many families with children and the children were few in number. A fair amount of the other families consisted of siblings living together. Plenty of the occupants were miners, but some did odd jobs around the town or helped the farmers with their crops and livestock and a few others volunteered as Watchmen. The people who weren't miners didn't really make money but given the town's general need for self-sufficiency, they got along by barter, trading work and favors among themselves for what they needed.

The Wyatt family was Grimluk and Sadie's first stop. Bray, the youngest, greeted the pair at the door, presenting himself as the mouthpiece for his family. The trio of brothers were miners and looked it in

every sense. Each man had a beard that every mountain man and dwarf could respect, if not envy, and
their bodies were thick with the kind of muscle that
comes from heavy work.

Bray shook Grimluk's hand and nodded to Sadie.
"Ma'am." Dark hair draped across his shoulders. He
was the shortest of them all but only in comparison
to his brothers, and now Grimluk himself. Bray still
stood over those of average height.

The eldest, Luke, stood almost as tall as Grimluk.
His hair was black, thinning at the crown, and graying.
His eyes shown with an intensity few could stomach.
Grimluk met and held that gaze, nodding his head to
the man. Luke nodded slowly in return.

The middle brother, Erick, stood at eye level with
Grimluk. The man's head was shaved clean but his
beard was just as long as his brother's and red. He
remained silent, not greeting their guests. Instead, he
observed everything from behind them.

"Welcome to our humble home," Bray started. "I
assume you'd like to get down to business immediately?"

Grimluk looked between the brothers. "I would."

"Well, please," Bray started, "join us in the drawing room." He motioned dramatically for his guests to
make themselves comfortable in one of few chairs in
the front room. Laughter filled him as he did so.
Before Sadie could sit, he offered her a rocking chair.
"This was sister Abigail's." The tone was reverent but
distant. "She loved this chair." A huge smile drew
across his face.

"Thank you, Bray," Sadie replied with a smile of
her own. He made her uneasy but she smiled all the

same. It helped that the rocker was easier for her to climb.

"If you could start at the beginning," Grimluk suggested, settling into the chair he assumed Erick frequented, "tell me when you noticed that things weren't right, what you experienced, what you're currently experiencing. Any other details you think could help me are welcome as well."

Bray shook his head in agreement. "Of course. The beginning is the only way to start." The young man began to recount their experiences. He claimed his brother Erick had been ostracized after being found one morning wearing a sheep's face. The animal's mutilated remains spread out at his feet. Grimluk looked toward the middle Wyatt. Erick returned his gaze. Bray continued on, pacing in a small circle, telling them how Luke had begun seeing things he shouldn't have been able to. How he said his skin had begun to itch in strange places and how, finally, he had howled, swearing that dozens of pale eyes had begun forming all over his body. Grimluk noted the man's bare arms showed no signs of scarring or wounds and only the two eyes at present.

Erick and Luke both looked on at their brother as if spellbound. Luke's eyes, intense to begin with, were now wide and unblinking. Erick's face was an emotionless mask. Bray's words were growing to a fever pitch, railing against the town itself as their true enemy. "They allowed the thing to infest our lives and then judged us for it!" he shouted.

An almost inaudible rumble formed in Grimluk's throat but he said nothing, letting Bray continue on. The young man's words took on an air of incoherence. He blamed the Watch and Kenton Selbie and the two previous demon hunters. Finally, he turned to Grimluk.

"I pray, friend, that you are no pretender, no charlatan. I pray you speak true when you say you mean to save us." Bray locked eyes with Grimluk, never wavering even as Grimluk stood. Bray didn't move an inch.

Grimluk extended his hand to Bray. "I speak true, Mr. Wyatt."

Bray seemed to measure Grimluk, with a smile ultimately spreading across his round face, laughter filling him as he took the hand and shook it hard. Grimluk noticed Bray seemed to deflate some in that moment.

"Thank you for your time, Mr. Wyatt," said Grimluk. "I think that's all I need."

"If you need anything else, please, don't hesitate to return," Bray offered.

Grimluk nodded. Sadie slid out of the rocking chair and followed him back outside. The pair's second stop was a father and his son, Rhim and Ajay. They were brown-skinned elves with shaggy mops of black hair falling over their pointed ears. Rhim's honey-brown eyes were bloodshot. Ajay refused to look anyone in the eye.

They were quiet and polite but short with Grimluk. Rhim was visibly hesitant to speak with them. His body language told Grimluk he was wound up enough he wanted to bolt. Sadie saw she needed to step in, as Grimluk had told her all too well, and persuade Rhim to talk. She was surprised when her simple confirmation that Grimluk was there to help allowed Rhim to relax some. The man clearly needed some sleep but he relaxed enough to talk.

Most of what they'd been through had happened fairly recently. They had paid no mind to the cycle of nightmares at first but at some point, the nightmares refused to stay in their dreams and invaded their waking lives.

Rhim had jolted awake from a particularly disturbing dream involving a man in a red coat luring Ajay away. He'd decided to go check on his son but his heart had frozen when he slipped into the bedroom. Ajay was gone. The window was open. Rhim took off for the Watch. Despite the night Watch's best efforts, he had demanded that Trilgor inspect the scene personally. The Watch captain followed him, armed, ready, and very much wanting to know where a teenage boy could disappear to in such a small town. There was no disappearance though. Rhim and Trilgor scared Ajay half out of his skin. The window was closed and the boy had clearly been sound asleep.

A few days later, Ajay woke in the middle of the night to the man in the red coat tapping at his window. Ajay had told his father that it looked something like an ogre but smaller, man-sized. The face was long and gaunt with a huge and grotesque jaw. Rotten teeth filled the man's huge mouth. Orange eyes locked onto the boy's as a sonorous voice beckoned Ajay to come with him. Ajay had screamed. The whole building bolted awake.

Ever since, the thing in the coat had been torturing them both. If it wasn't tapping at Ajay's window, it was appearing at the foot of Rhim's bed to tell him of how he would feast on the boy. Flesh and soul consumed in a banquet of eternal pain.

Grimluk let himself out as Rhim broke down

into tears. A few minutes later, Sadie joined him, her own eyes looking watery. She sighed deeply. "Is this what you always have to deal with?" she murmured.

"Yes. Maybe not this exact thing, but yes."

"How?"

"By finding the thing causing it all and stopping it." He looked down at her with concern, wondering if he shouldn't just forge ahead without her. "When you're ready, we can continue. Or you can leave and I'll continue on my own."

Sadie looked up at him, seeing his concern plainly. Her chin quivered as she thought about what else she might hear but she held the tears back. "You're a good person, Grimluk."

A small smile crept to his lips. "I try."

As the day wore on, they spoke to dozens of people. Or tried to, at least. The lack of anything resembling meaningful rest along with frayed nerves had worn the residents of Greenreach Bluffs down thin. Everyone was jumpy. Grimluk did his best to show them all compassion while still coaxing information from them. No matter how sincere the compassion, a few of the families saw him leave with little more details than he'd started with. He was grateful Sadie was with him. For her part, Sadie would help ease worry with her familiarity, sometimes reminding them that she suffered as well.

A brother and sister, dwarves, tan from helping the farmer and animal wrangler, brown hair speckled with sun-bleached highlights, argued about the interview at first. It took some doing but Sadie persuaded them to talk. After a long silence, they told Grimluk not of nightmares but of seeing things. Sometimes the strange visions happened under the blazing sun as they worked. Thorill, the brother, mentioned spiders. He tugged on his short beard as he gathered his thoughts.

"They come crawling out thin-air," Thorill said with a resigned sigh. "And they're big. I'll be tending the goats and look away and then, out of the corner of my eye, a huge fucking spider, white as a cloud crawls over one of the goats and then it's gone when I look. Sometimes, I see them comin' from the ceiling as I'm tryin' to sleep."

His sister, Threya, with braided mutton-chops, swore up and down that every time she tended the greenhouse, the plants grew and threatened to strangle her. Like her brother, she'd see it out of the corner of her eye, creeping vines unfurling and grasping for her. Then nothing. Both of them said they would occasionally wake in the night to see a shadowy figure hovering over the other while they slept. The revelation surprised them both, as they hadn't shared that detail with each other.

Grimluk and Sadie also visited two elf women and their adopted, human daughter. The elves, Lellala and Rhilda, had chestnut hair, and sparkling eyes with bags under them. Lellala's eyes were sky-blue while Rhilda's were ash gray. Their daughter, Maria, was a petite four year-old with bouncy, blonde hair and olive green eyes. Maria hid behind Rhilda as her mothers explained that, strangely, they had never had any nightmares or weird experiences. Maria, however, had been plagued by nightmares for almost a year.

"Most nights are bad nights," Lellala began.

"Maria dreams these horrible things up, terrifying, giant bugs."

"We go into check on her, and you'd think we'd be used to that by now," Rhilda said with a sigh, "but every night it happens, she climbs one of us like a tree, screaming for us to get off the floor or they'll get us."

Grimluk heard a small, soft sob from behind Rhilda. Maria had started to cry a little. He went to his knee. "Hello, Maria. I'm here to help you. Can you tell me more about what happened to you?"

"Demon bugs on the walls," she said meekly, her lips not fully coordinating with the words yet. "They're mean and big and wanna eat us." She moved, cautiously, towards Grimluk. "Can you make them go away?"

"I think I can. That's what I'm here to do. It might take me a little bit, but I'm going to try, okay?" She nodded slowly at him. An idea came to him. "You know, sometimes I have bad dreams too."

"Really?" Maria asked, wide-eyed.

"Mhm. And there's a phrase I use when I have bad dreams. Maybe it'll help you too," he offered.

"What is it?"

"Well, first, you have to shout at them, command them. You say, 'Demons!' Can you do that?" She squeaked the word. "Oh, you can do better than that. Try it again."

Maria moved from behind Rhilda now and took a deep breath. "Demons!"

"Yes, good girl, just like that! Then you say, just as strongly, you say, 'Klaatu! Berada! Nickto!' Give it a try."

"Klaatu! Bearda! Neckil!" She looked at him with a smile, waiting on his approval.

"Very good," Grimluk said with a grin. "Those demons better watch themselves. You just say that whenever you feel scared and have bad dreams."

Maria nodded enthusiastically. Her mothers looked at Grimluk with gratitude and thanked him. He thanked them for being so accommodating before leaving.

After that, a young human man and his fiance begrudgingly related how he'd been in one of the apartment outhouses late one night as something tried to break in. How it had snarled and bashed the door so hard he was sure the iron latch would rip free and the door would crush him before whatever it was ripped him to shreds. A few minutes later, it had stopped. Since then, he couldn't go use the outhouse at night. When he'd tried, he'd felt something watching him, waiting. His legs moved on their own when that happened and he was back inside, panting and dazed.

Some people reported rather mundane sounding but intense dreams. One halfling woman reported a constant series of dreams about people chasing her. Sometimes it was people she knew would never harm her, while other times, it was people who had tried or succeeded in hurting her. The dreams seemed to last all night, leaving her drained and understandably exhausted. She had begun going to sleep later and later.

"Things seem to be going, er, well," Sadie commented after leaving the halfling's apartment. The stories weighed on her but she was glad people seemed to be attempting to be forthright.

"Well, hopefully that little show I put on had-" Grimluk's head jerked away, his ears straining for a moment. He grunted. "Had helped."

"What was that?"

"Thought I heard something. Anyways, shall we continue?" He knocked on the next door. After a minute, and no answer, he knocked again. Still no answer. He turned the doorknob and the door cracked open a little before bumping into something behind it. Grimluk looked at Sadie.

"I don't know." She shrugged.

"Who lives here?" Grimluk asked.

"Um...Joseph Bartlett, I think."

"Joseph," Grimluk said through the cracked door, "I'm Grimluk. I'm here with Sadie to talk to you about your experiences with the demon." Silence. He pushed on the door a little more and could hear the sound of the wood scraping against something softly. He frowned and pushed hard, moving the door inward. The walls were covered in drying, bloody symbols, most of which resembled a tilted question-mark, with another, curling line through the dot that hooked underneath itself. Joseph's corpse lay behind the open door.

The color drained from Sadie's face. "I'll go get Trilgor." She was out of the door before Grimluk could respond.

Chapter 7

After finding Joseph's suicide, Sadie suggested they finish up for the day. She was emotionally spent and dinner time was approaching. Grimluk promised this would be their final interview for the day. Sadie sighed and agreed. Grimluk reached out and knocked on the door. The footsteps were barely audible before the door swung open. Looking up at them was Gwen, the little girl that had greeted him outside of Jhaan's store. Her eyes grew wide as excitement filled her small frame. She squealed, "Mr. Orc!" Her mother came to the door to see what the commotion was.

"Oh, you're here." She seemed to frown. "Um, come in."

Mother and child moved away to let their guests in. Grimluk entered, tipping his hat. Sadie following behind. The main room looked like all the others they'd seen. The only variations tended to be furniture placement but sometimes even that was the same. The pair moved away from the door. Gwen beamed up at him.

"Hi, Mr. Orc, hi Miss Sadie," she said with a great big smile.

"Hello, little one." Grimluk gave her a half smile.

"Hi there, Gwen," Sadie replied in turn.

"And hello to you too, miss..." Grimluk extended his hand.

"Missus Quinn." She hesitated before shaking his hand. "Cassie."

"Grimluk."

"My husband, Peter, is on duty. Actually, you two apparently met already."

"The Watchman."

"Mmhmm. He won't be back for a few hours still. Is that alright?"

Grimluk nodded. "That's fine. I can talk to you and the children and find him later." He felt a tug on his coat and looked down at Gwen. He knelt down in front of her. "Yes, little one?"

"I like your teeth," she said, pointing at his tusks.

"Thank you, very much. You know, orcs take special pride in their teeth." He gave her a big tooth-filled smile. "Strong teeth are very important. I hope you're taking care of yours so they can become strong like mine." Gwen shook her head with great enthusiasm as he stood back up. She continued to smile up at him. He looked at Cassie again. "Is your son here too? Nicholas, wasn't it? You can tell us what you and the children have been through. Or, if it would make you more comfortable, I can talk to you privately first and then the children. If you like, and she's willing, Sadie could keep up with the children outside while we talk."

Sadie nodded. "I don't mind, Mrs. Quinn."

"No, no, it's alright. Nicholas should be home soon. He likes to go for walks sometimes. I don't really like it, what with everything but he says it helps him feel better. He gets upset if I don't let him go."

"Alright. I'll try to make this as quick as I can, Mrs. Quinn." Grimluk sighed. "I know this isn't the most comfortable of topics. Just find the most comfortable place to start if you like."

Cassie looked back and forth at Grimluk and Sadie. She closed her eyes and took a deep breath. "Alright." She turned. There were two larger wood chairs near the wood stove that served for cooking and heating. Two smaller chairs sat nearby. She sat down in hers. "Nicholas seems to have had it worst. He was always quiet but now he's more withdrawn, especially after he's been drawing the strange things he draws. I think he doesn't want to worry us, so he stays quiet. I don't know. Maybe you can get something more out of him when he gets back. He doesn't like to talk about any of it."

Gwen had taken a seat in the small chair next to her mother as she spoke.

"Gwenny," Cassie started, looking down at her daughter.

"It's okay, Momma."

"Gwenny's had some bad dreams but mostly, she sleeps fine. But...she says things sometimes. It doesn't sound like her. And she says the most awful things. Sometimes she remembers, sometimes she doesn't."

"What kind of things?"

"Horrible things about people dying. If we're out, she'll just stop and look at someone and tell them they're going to die and how." Cassie's frowned heavily. Gwen gently patted her mother's arm.

"Momma," she said very gently, "can I talk to Mr. Grimluk by myself?"

Cassie looked at Gwen for a long while. "Are you

sure, sweetie?"

Gwen nodded and kissed her mother's forearm. "I can do it."

Cassie looked up at Grimluk with a mother's protective eyes. He gazed back. "Okay, Gwenny."

Gwen stood from her chair. "Okay," she said with all the authority of her tiny body. She walked over and took Grimluk's hand, which was almost big enough to take hold of her whole arm, and led him to a doorway, one of two, at the back of the main room. Inside was her and Nicholas's shared bedroom. She ushered Grimluk inside before she closed the door gingerly behind them. The room had beds on either wall, two small dressers and a lone window. Gwen climbed up on her own bed.

"Mr. Grimluk, I have to tell you a secret," she whispered.

"What would you like to tell me?"

"I didn't want to tell Momma, but I saw you in my dreams last night." Her face was very serious.

Grimluk's throat rumbled lightly in thought. He knelt down. "What did you see, little one?"

"I think I saw you burning everything. Everyone was crying and upset and it was scary. I don't know if it was right though. You're not scary, Mr. Grimluk, so I didn't tell Momma."

"I appreciate that," he said with a nod, "that might've made my job more difficult. Can you tell me what else you've seen and how you feel when you see these things?"

"I saw," she paused in thought for a moment, "I saw people in trouble and hurt and dying. Mr. Mayor was in some of the things. And brother. Brother's in my dreams a lot but he's scary and mean. A long time ago, I dreamed he was the demon and he put something in my head. I guess it was the demon though and that's why I tell people bad things. But I saw brother all in red and Mr. Mayor was near you with the fire." Gwen looked down at the floor for a moment. Her small body shivered hard for a moment and then she looked back up. Her eyes had gone black and glassed over.

"I see death and despair, Orc," she said in a voice both her own and not her own. It sounded like someone was speaking in unison with her. The other voice fluctuated heavily, seeming to change with each word while Gwen's voice remained stable.

"I see blood pooling under corpses. I see maggots writhing in old wounds. I see parents eating their children and children eating their parents. I see eaters of carrion filling the town. I see everything to come. I see the end of life. I see the end for you."

Gwen's body shivered hard again, her eyes and voice returning to normal. "I saw lots of bad things like that, Mr. Grimluk. At least, that's what I can remember."

Grimluk nodded and gave the child's knee a light pat. "Thank you, little one. That was very helpful. Is there anything else you remember?" She shook her head. "Okay. Let's go back to your mother."

Gwen slid off her bed. She neared the door, about to open it but stopped and turned back towards him. "Mr. Grimluk, can I have a hug?"

He looked at the little human girl with a note of surprise, still down on one knee. "Alright."

Gwen walked over and wrapped her arms around

the hunter's neck. He put one arm around her, all but swallowing her up. She let go, turning around once again to open the door. She disappeared out of the doorway, her little feet pattering back into the main room. "Momma, we're done. Mr. Grimluk said I was very helpful."

Grimluk stood up, great worry furrowing his brows. The child had been unaware of the words very clearly spoken through her. He made his way back into the front room slowly, pondering the purpose of the thing's words. Whatever demon was terrorizing the town could be the one speaking through Gwen. If that was the case, was it testing him now? He would press on, of course, but the thought burned in his brain. If it wasn't the demon though, what was it?

As Grimluk stood in the front room of the Quinn's dwelling, pondering, the front door opened and in came Gwen's brother, Nicholas. He didn't notice the hunter at first, as he turned to shut the door. Then he turned back and saw the hulking form and dark coat and froze. The boy's eyes were ice as he studied the hunter. Likewise, his face was blank. He gave a sniffle before walking past Grimluk. He grinned inwardly at the boy's poker face.

"Momma, what's he doing here?" Nicholas inquired with a quiet monotone.

"You know why he's here, we talked about it after the Watchman came by. He just wants to ask you about the things you've gone through. I'm sure he'd like to ask you about that now if you're okay with it."

Nicholas stood quietly, ignoring Grimluk, before shrugging with indifference. "Okay."

"Would you prefer to talk here or privately?" The

boy shrugged. Grimluk took him in, his mind working through the situation. "Alright," he answered. "Tell me about what you've been through. Your mother says you won't talk to her. I hope you'll speak to me now so I can help you and your sister."

Nicholas stared at the hunter with a cold resistance. His face tightened in thought. "Bad things," he finally said with a sigh. Some of the coldness seemed to melt off. "Monsters. Sometimes Gwen would disappear. Sometimes I come to while drawing strange things. Sometimes." The boy chewed on his bottom lip for a moment. His gaze wandered towards the floor.

"Go on..."

"Sometimes, Momma and Daddy would be dead." He took a deep breath and let it out slow. "I don't wanna talk anymore," he murmured, his gaze still on the floor.

Grimluk watched the boy for a long moment. "Would it help if we talked alone?"

"No," Nicholas replied, the icy monotone returning to his voice.

"It's very important you tell me things in detail. Maybe you could show me what you drew. Your sister was very helpful to tell me everything she could."

Nicholas's face turned up, once again peering at Grimluk's dark eyes. His mouth twitched. His gaze left the hunter's and fell to his sister before returning back to Grimluk. Silence. As Grimluk was about to speak again, a curious look spread across the child's face. Inquisitiveness filled his eyes.

"Have you ever killed anyone?" he asked the hunter with sudden, full attention.

"Nicholas!" Cassie responded in bewilderment. "Why would you ask something like that?"

"I'm just curious, Momma. He's asking me questions, why can't I ask him some?"

Grimluk met the woman's confused eyes and nodded at her. Cassie sighed and returned to preparing their dinner. Grimluk returned his attention to Nicholas. He held the boy's gaze, letting an uncomfortable silence build. Nicholas shifted his feet and looked away. His eyes shifted down towards the hunter's hip.

"You must've. I reckon you've had to kill bandos."

"Bandos?" Grimluk's eyebrow cocked in bemusement.

"Yeah, bandos. The people who attack people out on the roads."

"Ah. I think you mean 'bandits.' And I try not to kill."

"So you've definitely killed people then."

"Maybe," Grimluk replied after a long pause.

Nicholas chewed on his thumbnail in thought. "Can I see your gun?"

Grimluk saw Cassie start. She turned towards them again. Gwen stood next to her, looking up as well. He held up a hand to Cassie as a signal that it would be okay. He gave Gwen a little wink. Nicholas looked back at his mother and sister.

"If I let you see it, will you bring me any of the drawings you still have or remake them if you can remember? I'd like to study them."

"Yeah, okay." Nicholas's eyes were locked on the hunter's hip.

Grimluk pushed his coat back and drew the huge revolver, holding it broadside out, his trigger finger straight out. The boy took in every detail of the dark metal he could. He reached out to touch the runes along the barrel. Grimluk grunted and slid the revolver back into its holster, drawing his coat back over the weapon to conceal it once more. Nicholas looked incredibly disappointed.

"Now then," Grimluk started, "I would appreciate it if you would go make those drawings for me, Nicholas."

The boy's face contorted for a moment. "Now?"

"Yes."

Nicholas disappeared down the hallway towards his and Gwen's bedroom. Twenty minutes later, he returned with a few pieces of paper and shoved them up at the hunter. "Here they are," he said briskly, holding out the small stack of papers. "Can I touch your gun?"

Grimluk took the drawings from the boy's small hand. "No. I'm sure your mother would not appreciate that at all." He looked over at her. She silently mouthed, "thank you," and sighed. "Thank you for your help, little ones. I'll leave you be now. I think I have everything I need for the time being."

"Bye, Mr. Grimluk," Gwen shouted.

"Bye, little one. Thank you again, Mrs. Quinn."

"Tomorrow is Peter's day off. If you want to speak to him, you could come back then," Cassie offered.

"I just might."

Cassie nodded at Grimluk and waved to Sadie as the pair made their way back out of the Quinns' home. Sadie closed the door behind them. "So now what?" she asked.

"Now, I look at his drawings and eat. I appreciate your help. You're welcome to join me," he said as he tucked the drawings into his bag.

"I think I'll just go home and make some tea," she said. "And as long as you don't come knocking down the door again, I'll keep helping," she said with playful annoyance.

"No promises. Doors are fragile things," he replied in jest as they parted ways back on the street.

Grimluk returned to the Silver Sliver. He made arrangements for food and ale and returned to his room. After putting his things down, he sat and waited on his dinner, contemplating on all the information he'd gathered that day.

His food arrived shortly and once he was alone again, he pulled out the drawings. He flipped through them in between bites of food and gulps of ale. A couple of the pages were lots of circles and triangles with curved lines cutting in and out, each of them separate. Grimluk frowned at them, thinking they looked more like hasty scribbles than drawings from a trance. One page made him reconsider this stance though.

"A summoning circle?" Grimluk murmured to himself in surprise. He took a lazy bite of chicken as he studied the sign and his throat rumbled in thought. The boy had obviously not been completely truthful about what he'd been through, which didn't surprise him. It wasn't the first time.

He recognized a few of the runes but then others were alien. He did his best to try and recall seeing them anywhere else but it was no use. He finally set the pages back down, ready to finish his meal. He picked up a tankard and downed it before leaning back in thought.

It was time to talk to Ivor again. He would need help deciphering the circle's true purpose, if any, and surely the old magician knew more about magical symbols and signs than he did. Or at the very least, had information about them that he could reference. Grimluk took off to see the old magician.

"I need your help."

"It's nice to see you again too," Ivor remarked with a laugh.

"With this." Grimluk held up the page. Ivor took the drawing, his attention caught, and inspected it. "The Quinn boy, Nicholas, said he would occasionally come to while drawing strange things. Most of them look more like a child's scribblings, but this one, obviously, does not. I only recognize a few of the symbols on it though. I was hoping you would know what it was and what it might be for or might have a book that could show the way."

Ivor nodded. "You're definitely sharper than the other two," Ivor mused. "I don't even remember them asking if anyone had actually *seen* a demon wandering the town. But sure, I can look it over. You're welcome to stay or you can leave the drawing with me and come back tomorrow."

"I'll leave it with you," Grimluk said with a nod. "Maybe you can help with something else too..."

"What's that?"

"Selbie."

"Ah, our right honorable mayor. What about him?"

"Do you know him well?"

"Hm, not well enough to be much help. You've seen his behavior for yourself."

Grimluk's throat rumbled in response. "My gut says there's something more going on with him. Beyond his *clearly* abundant concern for the town's continued existence. Did you hear about the 'test' he pushed on me?"

"Truthfully, I was sound asleep but I heard he made you fight a ghoul."

"It wasn't a ghoul. At least, not one I'd ever seen. It was the elf, Ald'n, the last hunter. He was dead, yes, and he even reckoned that fact, but he didn't *look* dead for very long. All the decay disappeared and he healed from any blow I gave. Put my knife through his skull and he shrugged it off and pulled it back out. And if that weren't bad enough, Selbie was completely in control. I suspect through the strange amulet he had on. Ald'n wanted to take a swing at him and the good mayor halted him."

Ivor stroked his beard. "Amulet, hmm? I don't know anything about it but I do know that it has to be recent. Selbie's never had anything like that for as long as I've known him. I suppose it's possible he's been hiding it but I doubt it. When you've worked in magic long enough, you get a feel for it. I'd wager you understand that all too well though, am I right?"

"Perks of the job. I guess I need to get some more answers then."

"I certainly hope to have at least one for you

when you return."

Grimluk gave the old magician's shoulder a pat. "I'm grateful for the help." Ivor nodded. "I'll be back tomorrow. If you stumble over anything concerning amulets that make ghouls, be sure to save that as well."

Ivor bowed his head. "Hopefully fortune smiles on us."

Grimluk bowed his head in return before heading back out into town. He stood outside for a few minutes, taking in the air and ordering his thoughts. He needed answers but he'd have to plan smartly to get them. Kenton Selbie had shown nothing but deception. Grimluk had no doubt he would continue that trend.

It had been a long day and he hated to do it but he decided he would have to press Sadie some tonight. With a sigh, he made his way to the mayor's gate. This time, upon arriving at the door, he used the doorknocker. He plucked it up between his index finger and thumb and moved it back and forth several times. The metal clinked on its base but resonated enough that it would be audible.

Surprise covered Sadie's face as she appeared behind the door. Even still, she was much more pleasant this time. Her red curls were pulled back from her face and her sleeves were rolled up. Flour speckled her face and forearms. She had wiped her hands before opening the door. Grimluk motioned for her to step out for a moment.

"Not sure what's going on but at least you listened and didn't break down the door again," Sadie said, giving Grimluk a momentary grin. She pulled the door mostly closed.

"I listen on occasions when it benefits me," he replied with a half-smile.

"Well, what can I do for you?"

"I know. I'm sorry. I need to see your boss though." His face was stern. "We need to have a serious discussion."

"Now? Grimluk, it's been a very long day..." Weariness filled her voice.

"No, no," he replied. "Tomorrow evening. Alone. And I need to know more about his little toy from the test."

"The necklace?"

"It's an amulet. May be connected to the demon. If you can find anything out about it tonight, we can discuss it tomorrow. I'm sorry to ask so much of you."

Sadie sighed. "I'll see what I can find out."

"Thank you. I'll leave you be now. I'll see you in the morning, unless you'd rather not continue. You are more than right if that's how you feel."

Sadie more or less grunted at Grimluk, waving him off. "I'll be there. I just need some rest."

"See you tomorrow then," Grimluk said, nodding and heading back to the Sliver. Sadie slid back inside quietly with a heavy sigh. After a moment, she went back to her baking.

CHAPTER 8

Grimluk stood on the Silver Sliver's porch, basking in the morning sunlight. In an hour or so, the temperature would jump up but for the moment, it felt good and brought relief from a night of disturbed dreams, which had mostly faded from his mind now but the image of an army of imps stuck with him. The demon was beginning to get to him. Hopefully, he thought, Sadie would have something for him. He didn't want to grasp blindly with Selbie and the amulet. He could intimidate the man if he had to, and he probably would, but he preferred a more solid stance.

Grimluk waited. The sun ticked higher into the sky, bringing the heat with it. Sadie was nowhere to be seen. "Well shit," Grimluk muttered to himself. He sighed and rubbed the bridge of his nose for a moment, contemplating his next move. Across the street, he could see Wesson's silhouette in the back of the smithy. He had planned to speak to the miners today, but maybe he should re-plan for efficiency. Talk to the blacksmith first, check on Sadie, then see what Ivor found out about the summoning circle and finish the day interviewing miners. He considered, maybe foolishly, that if anything serious had happened to

Sadie, Trilgor would've already seen to it and informed him.

Grimluk's throat rumbled in thought. Might as well follow the simplest path. He stepped off the boardwalk and crossed the street. The smell of the forge met his nose as he entered. The smith, covered in a thick leather smock, looked up at him as he entered, his face wrinkling up into a scowl, his short, white beard twitching. As Grimluk approached, the older man very casually stood and moved towards him, a hammer in his right hand.

He saw the smith's body tense up. A half-second later, Grimluk threw both his arms out and to his left as the hammer came at him in a wide swing. The hammer flew away and slammed into the far wall. Without years of training and honed reflexes, his skull would've been in pieces in his brain.

Grimluk snarled. His strength had pushed the smith aside but he came back, throwing a punch now that his hammer was gone. Grimluk caught the smith's fist in his meaty, green palm, pushed it down, and took the old man's wrist in an iron grip. His free hand shot out and wrapped around the old man's throat, squeezing just enough to get the smith's attention.

"You have two choices, old man," Grimluk rumbled. "I let you go and we have a calm chat or I give a little squeeze and you take a nap. I'd prefer we talk."

The smith's eyes went wide, his face turning red with rage. "You piece of shi-," he began but Grimluk squeezed and cut the words off.

"I'm not. Trying. To hurt you." Grimluk eased his grip on the man's throat again.

The two stared at each other for slow minutes. The smith's face returned to its normal shade, his eyes remaining angry. He gave momentary thought of spitting in Grimluk's face but decided against it. He swallowed. "You think I'm some pissant weakling," he said with a snarl.

"I think you're an old blacksmith in a town being fucked with by a demon." Grimluk pulled his hand back from the man's throat and stepped back. "And I think we need to talk about that."

The smith stayed tense, opening and closing his fists repeatedly. Grimluk shook his head. The old man growled and spun away to track down his hammer. He came back grumbling. In one final expression of frustration and anger, he swung the hammer down onto the anvil as hard as he could. The sound of metal clanged out loudly, and the hammer's shaft snapped under the head, rebounding over the smith's shoulder and narrowly passed his face.

Grimluk stood quietly for a few minutes, letting the smith gather himself back up. He shuffled back to his chair behind the anvil and plopped back down. "Better?" Grimluk inquired.

"Fuck you."

"I'll take that as a yes," Grimluk said, crossing his arms. "Normally, I'd introduce myself and tell you to start at the beginning but today, let's go with why the fuck you decided I needed my brains bashed in."

The smith's hands clenched again, his nails digging into his thighs. He shifted in his chair before crossing his own arms as well, refusing to look up at the still silent Grimluk. "Ain't no law that says I gotta talk to you," he finally spat.

"That's truth. What reason do you have not to though?"

No answer. More stubborn silence as the smith stewed in his anger. He finally locked eyes with Grimluk. "I see the way ya look at me. I see the way they *all* look at me. You think the demon's made me weak. Made me soft. I ain't no fuckin sickly kid!"

Grimluk studied the man's face for a moment. "I never said you were a sick child. And I doubt that anyone else thinks that either. Everyone's too busy having fears and madness shoved down their throats to come up with shit like that. For fuck's sake, old man, I been here 'bout a week and it's starting to get to *me*. But then, I reckon I can kill this piece of shit with a hammer in my skull cause some old coot-," Grimluk stopped. He took a deep breath. "I'm sorry. This morning has been...taxing."

The old smith stared at him and seemed to deflate. The heat of his anger cooling. After a long moment, he sighed, and leaned over, propping his face up in his hands, elbows planted on his legs. When he spoke again, it was quiet.

"My name is Wesson," he finally said. "I was a sickly child. Nearly died from somethin' gettin' in my lungs. Nomunya, I think they called it. This...thing keeps replayin' those days. I keep wakin' up, small, and frail, and dying. Can barely keep the forge up, hardly even stitch a thin piece of leather. I see you walk in and I just...well look at ya! You ain't no frail weakling, are ya. Bet ya never been sick enough ya wondered if Death was comin' for ya."

Grimluk regarded Wesson's words. "I reckon not. This thing hasn't sapped you though. To my eyes, you would appear to remain a burly ol' cuss."

Wesson raised his head. Tears were welling up in his eyes. A moment later, the dam broke and the old smith broke down in great sobs. Grimluk looked on, his face etched in sympathy. He walked over to Wesson, gently patting one of his heaving shoulders. After a minute or two, Wesson's sobs lessened. He let out a great sniffle and a greater sigh.

"Thank you," Grimluk said quietly. "I'll leave you be." He began to leave but the old smith grabbed his arm. Grimluk turned.

"I'm sorry," Wesson muttered, letting go of the hunter's arm. "I'm sorry. Weren't right of me."

"Water under the bridge, friend," Grimluk said with a wave of his hand. "Besides, it takes a real hard ass to swing a hammer at an orc's face." He could hear Wesson give a little laugh as he left the smithy for the mayor's house. The man had clearly needed a release.

He arrived in front of Selbie's and slipped through the gate. He walked slowly up to the door, pausing for a moment before using the doorknocker. After a minute, the door opened and Sadie's face appeared. She was sweaty and out of breath, ringlets of hair stuck to her forehead. She frowned but said nothing. Grimluk sighed.

"You're okay." He paused. "Wait, are you okay?"

"I'm okay," she said quietly.

"No, you're not. What happened?"

"Mr. Selbie had tasks for me to do. I've been busy all morning."

"Tasks," Grimluk repeated back doubtfully.

"Yes."

Grimluk wanted to sneer. He took a breath to

compose himself. "I think it's time Selbie and I talk."

Sadie remained silent for a long time before finally moving to let him in. "Alright."

Grimluk stepped into the house, closing the door behind him. Sadie motioned for him to follow up the stairs. The wood creaked under his weight but held strong. The house was well made. At the top of the stairs was a three-way split. Each side was a small hallway that led into a bedroom. The middle door, which sat ajar, housed Selbie's office. Sadie approached it and knocked lightly.

"Yes?" Selbie answered distractedly from inside.

"Sir, Mr. Grimluk is here to speak to you."

"...tell him I'm occupied."

Grimluk put a hand to Sadie's shoulder and directed her away from the door. He walked in, letting his heavy step resonate.

"No, Mr. Selbie, you are not occupied with anything that cannot wait. We need to talk." He gave Sadie a nod before closing the door. She sighed as the door closed and went back to her cleaning. Behind the door, Kenton Selbie, surrounded by books in his leather back chair, stood up, trying to sound genial underneath his annoyance.

"Mr. Grimluk, I'd be happy to talk to you another time if you'd make an appointment. I am a busy man, whatever you may think."

"Sit," Grimluk commanded, fixing the man in his eyes. Selbie withered back down into his chair, looking very much like a scolded dog. Anger was still visible all over his now red face though.

"Mr. Selbie," Grimluk began, moving over to the sitting area. He took out his gun as he sat down, laying it across his lap. "Given what's going on with this town, I think we need to talk about that amulet of yours."

"If you're here to yell at me over your wounded pride at being tested-," Selbie began.

Grimluk held up a hand to silence him. "I'm here because your town is beset by a demon or some other evil. An evil that claimed two hunters prior to myself, one of which, *you* used to test *me*," he growled. "Now, the magician, Ivor says you've never had anything magical before. As far as my pride goes, what use is pride and bravado when you and your town need help? It doesn't help anyone. But you're running around with that amulet, which appears to be a fairly powerful piece of necromantic magic, and let me tell you one thing I've learned about necromancy in my travels."

He leaned forward slightly, holding Selbie's gaze tightly. The old man's body squirmed with agitation, but he couldn't look away from Grimluk's eyes. "The more power a living being has over the dead, the more likely it is to turn on them. And Mr. Selbie, that is a powerful bit of magic you have. What is it and why do you have it?"

Selbie continued to squirm in his chair, looking away from Grimluk. He remained quiet for a minute or two before sighing loudly. He put his face in his hands, elbows resting on his lap.

"I don't know *what* it actually is. It just showed up after the first hunter died. It had a note saying it could protect me from the dead and give me power over them. 'From a friend,' it said. I put it away after that. Then that other hunter showed up in town. He showed up at my door one night, said he'd followed something here.

"He barged his way into my house in the middle of the night, wanting to look around. He came in here and started throwing books around and going through drawers. I kept yelling at him to stop. Some of these books are old and very valuable. He wouldn't listen. He found the amulet in my desk and decided to take it with him. I tried to tear it away from him and he shoved me into the wall."

Selbie drifted off for a moment, growing silent. He looked like he had returned to that night. Anger and frustration and fear coloring his face. "He...I..."

Grimluk watched the old man's lip quiver slightly. Selbie looked back at him, into his black eyes. The old man's pale blue eyes were becoming red and watery.

"You have to understand, it was the middle of the night. He'd woken me up and was aggressive, I was scared, he was trying to make off with my property..."

Grimluk remained quiet. Merely stared at the old man impassively.

"I pushed him. Hard. As soon as my hands bounced off his back, I realized what I'd done..." The old man looked down at his lap. "I watched as he tumbled," he said quietly, "saw him dive headfirst into a step. I thought for sure he'd right himself, he's an elf, gods damn it! But he didn't and then he...his neck snapped so loudly when his body crashed into itself. There was blood and his skull was split open too."

Grimluk's nose wrinkled slightly. "So then you put on the amulet and put him where he'd be found later, blamed it on the demon." The old man nodded. "No wonder he wanted to rip your throat out."

Selbie's head snapped up at this comment. He looked about to burst into tears but then his face contorted into anger. "What more do you want? You got your answers, what else could you want?"

Grimluk towered over the mayor. "I want the amulet. If for no other reason than to make sure you don't try to kill me and make me into a puppet like you did Ald'n."

Selbie stared up at Grimluk, his fists clenching and releasing, like he was struggling with some unseen creature. His hands finally went slack and he stood slowly. He shuffled over to his big desk, fumbled through a drawer, and pulled out the amulet. He looked at it, watching it dangle and twirl from his fingers by its leather cord. Selbie looked up at Grimluk again, his eyes clearly showing the struggle in his mind. Grimluk could plainly see the old man was thinking of putting it on and using its power again.

Kenton Selbie nearly jumped out of his skin when Grimluk snatched the amulet from his hands, settling the decision for him. The old man felt like his heart was about to burst from his chest and collapse on the desk. Grimluk remained quiet, putting the amulet into his pocket. Selbie sat down at his desk chair and laid his head down. He heard Grimluk move to the door. Heard the knob turn and the hinges give a small creak as it opened. Heard silence after that for what seemed like hours.

He looked up. Grimluk was looking at him with hard eyes again.

"I sincerely hope you buried Ald'n properly. I'd hate to have to come talk to you again."

Grimluk turned then and left, closing the door.

He walked down the stairs. Sadie made her way to the door at the sound of his steps. He opened the door and looked back at her over his shoulder.

"I wouldn't bother him for a while. Thank you, again, Sadie."

She nodded, a frown coming across her tiny face. Grimluk walked back out of the house and closed the door gently behind him. Sadie, hands held against her chest, looked up at the stairs. She heard a lone sob. She let out a breath and walked silently back to the kitchen.

Grimluk stood quietly just outside the gate, examining Selbie's amulet. It appeared to be bleached bone set into a silver backplate. In the center was a strange, purple gemstone that almost seemed to absorb light. He felt a strange pulsing of energy coming from the gem. Despite what he felt, he thought the amulet had a strange beauty to it. He pocketed it.

It was time to visit Ivor again and learn what the magician had discovered. The temple stood silent once more as he returned. Grimluk made towards Ivor's dwelling area, this time pausing just outside it to call his name. No answer. He waited a moment longer before heading in. Unlike their introduction, Grimluk did not find the portly old magician snoring in his bed. Instead, he found Ivor slumped over the table at the back of the room, surrounded by a number of thick tomes and bathed in the dim light of a large, nearly empty lantern.

Some of the books appeared to be very old. They varied mildly in color and size, though most of them had been bound in similar styles. Various shades of faded reds, greens, blues, and blacks held the contents of generations of magical studies and diaries.

Grimluk walked over to Ivor and gently shook the magician's shoulder. He started awake with a snort, raising his head slightly. He stood back, letting the old man wake. Ivor yawned and stretched before turning around to face Grimluk. He nodded a hello before yawning again and wiping the crust from his eyes.

"What did you manage to find?" Grimluk asked.

Ivor sat silently, his mind warming up. He turned back to the table and picked up the paper with the summoning circle, looking it up and down like he'd done for what felt like dozens of hours already. He turned back to Grimluk and held up the drawing.

"I found," he began, pausing again, "that this drawing is fucking bullshit. I spent a good ten hours going through every book on runes or related to runes, every one on summoning circles, and everything on sigils that I had, and ya know what? It's bullshit. Some of those symbols are gibberish and some of them are just random. The center just says 'delicious chicken.' Ten gods damned hours and all I learned was that this piece of shit says 'blah blah big blah blah grave blah blah delicious goddamn chicken.' It says nothing."

Ivor rubbed his face with his free hand in frustration. "I mean, it doesn't literally say 'delicious chicken.' It's more like 'prepared bird,' but you get what I mean. It's nothing. Either Nicholas was fuckin' with you, or we got more than one problem in this town."

Grimluk rumbled in thought, staring at the page. Why would a kid give him a fake circle, he wondered. Even more puzzling, how did the child even know any of this to begin with? He took the sheet from Ivor. "I think that this boy warrants further questioning."

Ivor nodded in agreement. "Good luck with that. If you need me, I'll be in bed." The old man climbed out of his chair and collapsed into his bed.

"You're sure this is all you could find?"

Ivor responded with a muffled but still audible, "yes."

"Thank you, Ivor."

The old magician merely lifted an arm in reply.

Grimluk made his way back outside. It was after noon now. The sun was high overhead. A few wispy clouds floated high up. He crossed his arms and leaned back against the outside wall of the temple's entryway. He needed to figure out the best course of questioning for Nicholas. He still needed to speak to the boy's father, Peter, as well.

He walked slowly and very deliberately back towards the center of town, attempting to sort out the details of the situation thus far. After days of quiet, with barely any activity, there were a few people out now. He nodded to them as they walked past. His feet brought him over to the general store's porch where he sat down for a moment under shade of its awning. He watched as Thomas, the halfling, and a dwarf entered the Silver Sliver. They both seemed to be in better spirits.

As Grimluk sat, he heard the pattering of tiny feet running off to his left. Gwen appeared from the side of the building, kicking up a little dust cloud under her feet. Her faded little green dress twirling with her movements. Following shortly behind her was her mother. Gwen stopped and looked up, spotting Grimluk.

"Mr. Grimluk!" she squealed, a huge smile spreading across her tiny face. She raced over to him.

"Hello, little one. How are you?"

"Gooooood. Whatcha doin?"

"Having a nice think. What about you?"

"I tore my dress, see?" She turned and showed him the big hole in the back. "Momma wanted to fix it but was out of dress stuff."

"I see. Hello again, Mrs. Quinn."

Cassie waved politely. "Hello, Mr. Grimluk."

"Your daughter tells me you're out to buy fabric to patch her dress."

"That's right. I have no idea how she got that big hole in it," Cassie said with a sigh. Gwen gave a big, toothy smile.

Grimluk's laughed lightly at her expression. "She's welcome to sit with me while you shop. I don't mind the company." He gave Gwen a wink.

Cassie's mouth became a tight slit as she thought. "Are you sure?" she asked cautiously. "It won't take me long."

Grimluk gave a little wave of his hand. "She's good company."

Gwen stood in front of him, still beaming while she twirled and swooshed her dress.

Cassie nodded. "Alright. Gwenny, sit down with Mr. Grimluk and I'll be right back."

Gwen gave a little skip as she walked up the stairs, taking each step one foot at a time. She pattered over to the hunter and sat down next to him, dangling her minuscule legs over the edge of the porch. She absently swayed them back and forth. Cassie disappeared into the store.

Grimluk looked down at Gwen and patted her back lightly.

Her feet stopped moving and her body jolted, like it had in her bedroom. She turned her head to look up at him. The smile had faded and in its place was a placid expression. The neutral look was punctuated with black, glassy eyes however.

Grimluk's throat rumbled. "You again," he said quietly. "What are you? Why do you use the girl like this?"

Dual voices spoke to him in an eerie whisper, Gwen's little voice once more being shadowed by something clearly foreign. "Go out to the graveyard, Orc. Follow the outer wall towards the rock face. You will find answers there. And the doom you bring will march ever closer."

"Why do you tell me this?" Grimluk asked, his eyes narrowing and meeting the stark eyes of the child-not-child.

"Because you also bring salvation, Orc." Gwen's body jolted again. She looked back out towards the center of town as her legs began swinging again. Her eyes returned to their normal color. She looked up at him again, seeing a look of worry.

"What's wrong, Mr. Grimluk?"

"I guess I just have a lot on my mind, little one."

"Can I help?" she asked with the most sincere

look of sympathy he'd ever seen.

He looked into the child's eyes for a long moment. "Do you remember what you just said to me?"

"Did...did I say something bad again?"

"No, no, little one." He gave her head a gentle pat. "It may very well be of help. It's better you don't remember though."

Grimluk folded his arms across his chest, thinking on the spirit's words. He wondered what it was he would find outside the graveyard. He wondered what the spirit really was. Another demon? *The* demon? What was it and why had it taken up residence in Gwen's body? What part was it playing in everything? It seemed to present itself as an oracle of sorts. That, he thought, was bad news in and of itself. Oracles never brought good tidings. At least, none he had heard of.

The pair looked back as the door to the store opened and closed. Cassie stood with a small, brown bag.

"Ready, Gwenny?" Cassie said.

"Uh huh." She stood up. "Byyyyyye, Mr. Grimluk," she said as she followed her mother.

"Mrs. Quinn...Cassie, if it's still okay, I'd like to come by later and talk to your husband."

Cassie stood surprised for a moment. "Oh, yes, yes, of course but he's on duty again today. He won't be home til this evening. Someone got sick so Trilgor called him and Charlie in. You could talk to him now, I suppose."

"I see. Thank you, I may do that. If not, I'll ask him if I can stop by tonight."

Cassie nodded.

"Tell Daddy I said hi!" Gwen shouted.

Grimluk watched the two leave. Gwen waved emphatically as they rounded the building.

CHAPTER 9

Grimluk made his way towards the town's entrance. Peter and Charlie, the two Watchmen he'd met the day he arrived, were on duty. Charlie seemed a little more relaxed around him this time but that probably had to do with seeing Grimluk's fight with Ald'n. Grimluk touched his hat in greeting.

"Afternoon, friends."

"Afternoon, hunter," Peter replied.

Charlie gave a nod.

"Where are you off to?" Peter asked.

"I'm heading out into the desert. I got a bit of information that needs checking and it puts me outside the barrier."

The two Watchmen looked at each other a moment. "I see," Peter said. "Anything worth sharing?"

"You find the demon, maybe?" Charlie followed.

"Can't say yet. Not sure who gave the tip or whether it's even reputable. I saw your daughter and wife a little while ago, Mr. Quinn. Gwen says hello."

Peter smiled. "She seems to like you a lot."

"Seems to. I guess I have a way with the little ones," Grimluk said with a grin. "Anyhow, I was going to stop by and speak to you today but I think I'll wait til you've had dinner and I've had time to check whatever this is out."

"Oh, alright, sure. I guess I'll speak to you later then," Peter said with a nod.

Grimluk tipped his hat in thanks and passed between them quickly. The barrier hissed and popped as he slipped through. A stiff wind from the Wastes blew in, making Charlie jump as the hunter's coat tails snapped out. Her rifle whipped up to her shoulder.

Grimluk heard Peter yelp at his partner and turned around to see the rifle pointed at him for the second time. He held his hands up in peace. "Easy, Watchman."

Charlie sucked in a breath and lowered her gun. "S-sorry...sorry, Grimluk."

Grimluk lowered his hands, waiting a moment before resuming his path to the Greenreach Bluffs graveyard, following along a worn little path. As he walked off, Peter asked Charlie if she was okay. Gusts of wind blew up grit and dust and a sharp draft pushed on him. He wondered for a moment if something was trying to knock him over.

The graveyard was surrounded by a low stone wall about four feet tall, though it dipped down in places due to stones being uneven. It was still sturdy even with those imperfections. As he passed it, he noticed the iron gate was busted. It hung crooked and there was an indent in the ground from where the gate slid open. He turned at the wall's far corner and followed it back.

The graveyard itself was surprisingly quiet. All he could hear was the sound of a bird in the far distance.

Grimluk figured the magician worked to make sure Greenreach Bluff's dead didn't come back as ghouls, as he saw no movement from the graves. Each was as still as it should be. The gusts of wind shook the limbs of the few remaining dead trees. As he walked, natural dust devils whipped up every now and then before dispersing. Grimluk closed his eyes as he passed through one that sprang up next to him and moved over him, dying down as it did so.

He neared the back end of the wall finally. The very back wall was built up against the southeast end of the bluff as it began tapering out and back. It wasn't completely up against the bluff, but it was enough that you'd have to climb on top of the back wall to get around the rock. Grimluk scanned the area, stepping around the corner. He looked over the edge of the wall, behind an old tombstone, inspecting the area. Nothing but the desert floor and tufts of yellow weeds.

"Gwen's" cryptic words hung in Grimluk's mind as he surveyed the wall itself. He pushed on stones in the wall, looking for some sort of secret to reveal itself. A hidden cache of demonic scrolls, perhaps, or a worn symbol, an arrow to point the way. Nothing. He moved on to the outcrop of rock that sat, jutting out a few inches away from the back of the wall. He ran his hands over the stone, again checking for some hand-made indentation. He stooped down, running his hand over the underside of the rock. He felt nothing but rough stone.

What he heard was another matter. As the wind lulled, the low cry of a bird hit his ears. Grimluk listened again, swearing that it had come from under the rock itself. He almost missed the second cry as the wind blew again. It sounded hurt. Grimluk eyed the space under the rock. It went farther back but it was too small for him to get to it without crawling on his belly. Down he went.

The little hole led back a couple of feet into the cliff-face, opening up into a small hollow, not quite big enough to be a cave. It was big enough that Grimluk could rise up to his knees though, albeit with a lowered head. He closed his eyes tight in an attempt to expedite their adjustment to the low light. He blinked rapidly as he opened them again. The bird cried out again as he did so, louder now that he was so near it. He inspected the hollow.

Here were his answers. What appeared to be a small nest sat next to the wall with bones lined around it. The closer Grimluk got, the more he thought it looked almost like a little shrine. Snake skins were pinned around its border and the bones were arranged symmetrically, with a large bird skull pointing to the center. The bird cried out once more. He could hear the fear and hurt in it now all too clearly.

Grimluk half-crawled over to the would-be shrine to get a closer look. Sticks, feathers, and other debris lay scattered about, moving lightly. Grimluk pulled the big knife on his belt out, using the tip to push away the pile revealing the bird, a young dove. Its wings and legs were broken, and as it looked up at him in terror, they both flapped grossly in an effort to flee. The bird made a low noise at him when its fear subsided enough it remembered it couldn't move. Grimluk frowned, his brow furrowing. The bird would not survive even if tended to.

"I'm sorry, little friend," Grimluk said with audible remorse. A moment of expert precision ended the poor creature's suffering. He flicked the blood from the knife's edge before giving it a quick wipe on his coat and returning it to its sheath. Grimluk grunted to himself, looking down at the bird's corpse. He reached down and picked it up, laying it gently to the side.

"Damn it."

A chalk summoning circle sat where the bird had been moments ago. Grimluk pulled out the paper with the summoning circle on it and held it out to compare the two. They were the same.

He almost wished he'd caught the boy here. It would've assuaged the doubt that ate at him. There was no real proof that this was Nicholas's doing and he'd only been directed here by the spirit inhabiting Gwen. He wondered for a moment if he was being tricked by the spirit. His intuition said otherwise though and those same instincts had served him well through the years.

Grimluk thought on how best to broach this subject with the Quinns. Either their boy had summoned the demon or it had gotten in his head. Either way, the evidence couldn't be ignored. He crawled back out of the hole. As his eyes readjusted to the light, he realized suddenly that the sun was too low in the sky. There was no way he'd spent hours in the hollow but there was the sun, sinking into the horizon.

Grimluk shut his eyes tight. It had to be a trick by the demon. He summoned his will and calmed himself. He took in a deep breath and held it. His eyes opened and the breath released slowly. The sun had returned to its place high in the sky, resuming its normal path through the heavens. He began his return to town, hands in the pockets of his coat as he walked in thought, eyes on the path between Green-reach Bluffs and its place of rest for the deceased. A few minutes later, he looked up. The town was miles away. He turned around and the graveyard was just as far. The hardpan yawned out around him like an ocean.

"Seems I found a sore spot. Glad to see I got your attention," Grimluk said, not entirely without amusement. "Why don't you just show yourself and we can end this now."

Cruel laughter echoed on the wind.

Grimluk's gun snapped out, hammer cocked, as he sought his foe. As he scanned the infinite stretch of desert around him, a chill shot through his spine. The sun began to sink rapidly once more with frightening speed. Darkness closed in on him like an avalanche, sharp and cold and deathly. A sneer spread across his face. The gun slid back into its holster. Grimluk stood silently in a sea of shadow, trying to think of how to get free of the demon's power.

As Grimluk's mind raced, his stomach dropped suddenly, as if he'd taken a great fall. Laughter rose up once more on stygian winds, seemingly echoing all around him and through him, shrill and malevolent one moment and so cold and deep the next that it made his head throb. His guts tightened. His blood pumped ice-water. His legs clenched, eager to flee. Through an iron determination, Grimluk stood fast, willing his body calm. The laughter began to quiet, the echoes still cutting through his skull and the void around him.

Grimluk looked around, the only familiar sensation that of the wind which continued to blow. He grunted and then picked a direction and started walking. The laughter clapped out like thunder that seemed to echo for eternity. Grimluk's ears rang as he went forward. Each step as sure and confident as he could make them.

"Lost little goblin," came a sing-songy voice. The voice was lighter than the shrill laugh, a high whisper that sliced through Grimluk's mind with deafening insistence. He growled but kept walking.

"Oh, he doesn't like that, does he?" the voice asked in the same mocking cadence, the tone now considerably deeper. "Where are you going, little goblin?"

Light flashed far ahead of him. His feet shifted their aim and took him towards it. Two tall torches had lit up, burning in great, blue flames. Beyond them, another pair lit up. He kept walking towards them too. Then two more yet again farther ahead until he'd passed ten more pairs of torches. The final pair lit up the mouth of a cave. He noticed a change in the ground as his feet touched rock once more.

"Come, little goblin," the demon goaded in its sing-song tone again, "come and find me."

As Grimluk passed through the mouth of the cave, stone steps lit up, another bright blue flame billowing out before settling back down. The steps seemed, like everything else so far, to go on for eternity. He began to climb them.

"Who are you, demon?" Grimluk asked, hoping the thing was stupid enough to give its true name. His words were calm now that the thing was interacting with him. As far as he knew, if it wanted him dead, it could've ended him already.

"Goblin wants a name, yes, a name," the demon chided. This time, Grimluk heard the voice shift mid-word. The drop made his head swim.

"You may call us...Priskus, for we are ancient," it intoned.

"Cute," Grimluk mocked. The flames disappeared as he uttered this. His foot came down on air and he tumbled forward, head over heels. Startled, a yell slipped out of his mouth as he feel. Dust shot out from under him as he landed on his back. The impact shook every bone in his body, but he remained unharmed. More blue flames erupted in a circle around him.

"Such disrespect," Priskus bellowed so low Grimluk felt it more than heard it.

"I hunt your kind," Grimluk stated matter-of-factly, getting to his feet again, not bothering to beat the dirt off himself. "If you're lookin' for respect from a demon hunter then maybe your age is true and you've gone senile."

"WHELP!" Priskus screamed.

Instinctively, Grimluk covered his ears but it was futile gesture. The physical realm was gone but it felt like the demon's words were hard blows to his skull.

"I'd ask why you're here and why you seem to be bothering to palaver but I don't rightly give a shit," Grimluk spat. "Leave Greenreach Bluffs, demon, or you'll see just how disrespectful I can be." Grimluk stood up straight, looking around. Priskus remained silent. The surrounding blue flames began to die away until they puffed out.

"Orcs are never any fun," Priskus whined.

"Oh, I'm lots of fun. You haven't lived until

you've had a drunken brawl and a sing-a-long with me. But for you, maybe I'd be more fun if you showed yourself," Grimluk said defiantly. His coat moved back and he pulled his revolver from its home once more. "Or, I can make you."

"What?! What are you doing?!" the demon bellowed.

"You go pokin' around someone's head, sometimes they can go pokin' back." Grimluk concentrated and pushed his will out to the demon. The cavern began to rumble from the demon's growls as Grimluk reached out, pushing at the demon's mental connection.

A wall of flames erupted in front of him, illuminating the huge cave around him. Ahead of the inferno, Grimluk could see a huge, stone slab, with a tall, worn, stone statue behind it. They were hazy from the heat, as Priskus tried to fight Grimluk's attempt to see it. All he could make out was one, great, glowing eye from the statue's face and massive wings. It would have to be enough.

"So how about it, Priskus?" Grimluk challenged, pointing the revolver at the statue. "You gonna sulk or we gonna throw down?"

The demon hissed.

"Coward," he sneered. The gun roared and the statue's face shattered. Priskus roared with supernatural fury, bringing Grimluk down to one knee. "Cry all you want," Grimluk yelled back. "Either face me or end this!"

Priskus's roar bounced around the cave. As it began to die away, Grimluk heard a strange tick-tacking sound. The noise grew in intensity, echoing all around him. Animal screeches hit his ears. He looked up just as a group of black, leather-skinned imps came bursting out of a hole the ceiling. He counted eight, each of them screaming with hatred, before descending upon him. Little, yellow, pupil-less eyes glowed in the pale light.

The revolver sliced through the air as Grimluk aimed skyward. The gun barked and the huge bullet ripped through several of the creatures. Each one seemed to explode, guts, eyes, and claws flinging in every direction. Lumps of flesh fell to the cave floor with wet slaps.

Two more imps came at him from either side, having slid away on small wings just before their com-rades had become paste. Grimluk's huge body twisted. He used his own momentum to slam his fist into one imp as the other sailed past, crushing the tiny body of his would-be attacker. It flew away and bounced across the cave floor. Behind its corpse, more of its brethren spilled out of more holes in the cave wall.

Their numbers kept swelling. One bullet from his revolver would fell half a dozen or more at a time, smearing and splattering their bodies across the floor, the walls, the ceiling. After the sixth shot, Grimluk broke the chamber open, dumping the spent casings. The still smoking brass tinkled against rocked. His fingers worked as quickly as his adversaries would allow.

Finally, face and hands bleeding, Grimluk snapped the chamber shut. He struck out with the barrel and shattered the skull of an imp. Their num-bers had grown so large now that he didn't even bother aiming. He pointed and fired, each shot ripping through more of his attackers than he could register.

More than his gun now, all he could hear was the thunderous beating of what felt like thousands of membranous wings and the imps screeching with hatred, the maddening cacophony of thousands of tiny, razor-sharp nails scraping rock and his flesh. He bit, punched, headbutted, elbowed, and crushed anything that got near him. Blood flowed from every inch of him.

The imps were so thick now he could barely move. They clung to Grimluk in a cocoon of pain, claws digging into him, keeping hold as tiny daggers of yellowed teeth bit through cloth and flesh. One angry mouth found his throat. The skin and muscle slipped away like a windswept gossamer veil. Grimluk's throat gushed blood, cascading down the front of him, spilling over leather bodies. He sank down to one knee, grabbing his throat, fighting with all the intensity of a flickering candle about to snuff out. It was no use though. Grimluk collapsed, eyelids sinking heavily as his vision faded and the void swallowed him once more.

Moments later, his eyes cracked open. Moonlight shone down into his face through the dusty window of his room at the Silver Sliver. He laid in silence, his eyes blinking sluggishly and rolling in their sockets. He lifted his head to look around. His hat, gun, and bag sat on the small table, while he still wore his coat and gun belt. Grimluk reached up to rub at his eyes but winced. His skin screamed like every inch had been raked with jagged, hot coals, especially his throat. He grunted and took a deep breath. As he stared up at the dark ceiling, the pain began to ebb.

He sat up slowly. He was grateful to still be alive but wondered how he'd gotten back to his room. He'd clearly been out for hours.

Grimluk swung his legs over the edge of the bed and attempted to stand. Immediately, his head started swimming and he collapsed back down, feeling like he would vomit. He needed water but he had to pull himself back together enough to get it. He remained on the edge of the bed for maybe twenty minutes, trying to recover. Finally, after the pain and nausea had passed, he tried to stand again, slowly, wobbling for a moment as his feet returned to him. He stepped over to the table, grabbing his hat and gun. He donned his hat once more and then broke the chamber on the revolver, dumping the shells into his hand. All six still live and accounted for. He was relieved he hadn't been blindly firing during his afternoon excursion. The giant gun slid smoothly back into its holder.

Grimluk stretched for a moment, folding his arms behind his head to keep from scraping the ceiling, and then slipped out of the room quietly. He took slow, deep breaths as he took each stair-step, not wanting to play the fool and ignore the fatigue he felt. He couldn't help anyone if he was in a crumbled heap.

The saloon was almost as quiet as usual. Edgar was still sitting at his table playing his game. There were two halflings at the bar though sitting on stools. One of them was Thomas and the other a friend Grimluk hadn't met. They were having a low conversation, eating a late night meal. As Grimluk shambled over, they stopped talking. He nodded to Thomas as he stepped to the bar.

"Fuck, man, you look like shit," Thomas

observed.

Grimluk leaned on the bar. "Thanks."

Matthew, looking like a friendlier version of his father, stepped in front of Grimluk. "Thom's right. Charlie and Peter brought you in here hours ago and you were yellin' at somebody. The demon, we guess. You gave Peter a shiner."

Grimluk grunted. "You'd guess right. I'll have to apologize to Peter, buy him a meal. Right now, I could use some water though."

Matthew nodded and went to filling a tall glass from a pump. The young man sat the glass down. "Water's free," he said.

"Thanks," Grimluk breathed, picking up the glass. He took a few sips to test his head. His head and stomach remained even as he fought the urge to down the glass in one go. Matthew waited a moment but when Grimluk didn't look back up, he nodded lightly and plopped back down in the chair behind the bar. Grimluk closed as his eyes. He felt the water slide down into his stomach, cooling him from the inside.

"Sooooo...what happened?" Thomas's friend asked. He was chubby like Thomas, but had a narrow face and long, blond hair he kept tied back.

Thomas nodded emphatically. "Yeah, what'd you see? What happened? Did you find it?!"

Grimluk finished his water, lifting the glass and nodded to Matthew for more. A few moments later, Grimluk was sipping again. He hadn't quite realized how thirsty he was until the water hit his tongue.

"I found something outside of town," Grimluk said. "Something the demon didn't like given how hard the fucker came at me. Never showed itself though, just got in my head. It's strong."

Thomas and his friend looked at each other. They weren't sure what to think.

Matthew stared at Grimluk with concern all over his face. "I'd imagine so. The other two didn't fare so well against it."

Grimluk worked his jaw in thought, thinking about what Selbie had admitted to him. He looked over at the three faces watching him. With one smooth motion, he downed the rest of the water and stood up.

"Don't look so worried, fellas. If I had to guess, I'd say you're gonna see an orc punch a demon soon. Now, if you'll excuse me, I need to go speak to Ivor." As Grimluk headed outside he gave Thomas's shoulder a pat. He was starting to feel better now, more like his normal self. Once outside on Silver Sliver's porch, a light breeze brushed against him. He closed his eyes for a moment before heading towards the temple. The moon told him it wasn't as late as he felt it was, so the old magician would probably still be active.

Even though he was feeling better, the encounter with Priskus had still had an effect. The shadows made him uneasy. He kept moving though, arriving at the temple to find Ivor sitting at a table in the main chamber, sipping from a mug. The old man had his head buried in a large tome. He looked up at the sound of Grimluk's feet.

"I was wondering if you'd show up. Trilgor stopped in earlier, told me two of his men had carried you back into town."

"The demon decided to say hi finally."

The magician looked Grimluk over. His lips flattened together as his eyes squinted ever so slightly. "You seem to have recovered."

"Mostly," Grimluk replied. "The attack wasn't the whole of it though."

Grimluk pulled a chair back from the table and sat down gently, collecting his thoughts before he began to recount the afternoon's events. The old man listened quietly. After Grimluk had finished, Ivor sat, hand stroking his chin in thought.

"The girl is quite the anomaly," Ivor finally said. "Do you trust her words after finding what you did?"

Grimluk thought for a moment. "Trust is a strong word. The thing sounds threatening but..."

The magician nodded. "Regardless, it seems that Priskus is feeling pressured now. I'd say you're moving in the right direction given the intensity of your encounter. It took quite some time for anyone in town to experience anything close to that."

"Mm. I don't suppose the name is familiar?" Grimluk asked.

"No, aside from the clever little wordplay, I've never heard of a demon by that name. I could find a demonology book to be sure but as far as I know, the word is just a very old one meaning 'ancient.'"

Grimluk nodded. "I'd appreciate it if you could make absolutely sure for me. I'll pay you, if you require it."

Ivor waved a hand dismissively, sipping from his mug. "In normal circumstances, I protect this town. This has been mostly beyond me though. I know how to keep and maintain the barrier. I know how to med-icate and heal anyone who needs it. I can even defend myself, physically and mentally, if need be. Demon-fighting is beyond me though."

Grimluk stood and bowed his head to Ivor. "See what you can dig up on demon names." He slid his hands into his coat pockets idly. His face lit up. "And this," he said, dragging Selbie's amulet out. It twirled, the torch light glinting off the purple stone.

Ivor stared at the amulet, taking it gingerly from Grimluk's hand, standing up as well. "This is definitely necromantic in nature."

"Yeah, I'd think that's pretty obvious by now, wouldn't you?"

Ivor laughed. "I suppose you're right, hunter. I'll see what I can find on it. At least knowing what it does will help."

"Thank you again, Ivor."

The magician nodded, gathering up his book and mug before heading back to his room and books for more research. Grimluk wandered back outside and looked up at the moon. It would be full in a few nights. The pale light shone onto Greenreach Bluffs unobstructed. A rather large moth fluttered in front of his face, white as bone. For a moment, still recovering from the demon's attack, he thought it was huge and far away. It fluttered off to his right just as something moved from that direction. He turned as a shadow flickered though the moonlight, a small body slipping stealthily through the dark towards the mayor's house.

Grimluk moved towards the fence, keeping low and silent. The figure slipped through the gate, moving through the slim alleyway to the side of the house and disappeared into the darkness. He sat silent and still, trying to ascertain how he could track whoever it was. There was no way he could slip through that alley. As Grimluk sat on one knee in thought, soft steps approached from behind.

"What are you doing?" Ivor asked.

"I saw someone slip behind Selbie's." The thought abruptly occurred to Grimluk that it might have been Priskus screwing with his head again. He stood back up. "Maybe it was nothing."

"Well, no matter, you're here and I think I figured out something rather important. I remembered something after you left," the magician said. "Just hit me all of a sudden."

"I see. What is it?"

"The altar you saw, and the statue of Priskus, my master had written about an altar and statue the digging crew had stumbled upon when they first started tunneling. It was in one of his journals from before I was even born. I'd read all his journals after he died and it had suddenly hit me. The cavern was already there when they began."

"Did anything strange happen to anyone when they found it?"

"Nothing severe. A few of the diggers reported strange dreams and the chamber itself made everyone feel uneasy, especially seeing the statue but that was it."

"Where did this happen?"

"Outside of town. They sealed the tunnel up and everyone just forgot about it."

Grimluk's throat rumbled in thought. "Can we still get to it?"

"I s'pose. We'd have to get one of the miners and then figure out where exactly the damn thing is along the bluffs."

Grimluk nodded. "Alright, keep researching, find what you can on the demon or the amulet. If the tunnel's outside of town then we'll wait til daylight to inspect it."

"I'll look through the journals again too. And, you can have this accursed amulet back." Ivor shoved the thing out to Grimluk. "It makes my skin crawl just lookin' at it. I made a quick sketch of it and did a rubbing."

Grimluk took the amulet and stared at it. "I should probably just destroy this thing but without knowing more about it, I have no idea what that might do." He stuffed it back into his pocket. "I guess I'll meet you at the mine in the morning."

"Hopefully, you can find some rest tonight, hunter."

"Hopefully," Grimluk said with a nod as he headed back to the Silver Sliver.

Kenton Selbie sat alone in his sitting room, sipping tea and reading. The room was lit by three, tall oil lamps, one next to the chair for reading light. It flickered. He looked up at it and gave the knob a slight twist to no avail. The other lamps began flickering too.

"Selbie," Priskus called, drawing the old man's name out like a dagger.

Once more, Selbie watched as the light from the lamps dimmed unnaturally, drawing out every shadow in his house. The shadows swirled and came together, forming the vague shape of a person. A lone eye began to form in the center of the thing's face. It began to grow, glowing yellow and locking the old man into its gaze. He watched helplessly as it expanded beyond all rational measure, seeming to engulf his frail form. Minutes, or maybe hours later, he wasn't sure, the eye swallowed itself, as a malicious laugh rang in Selbie's ears.

Selbie groaned. "I wish you wouldn't do that."

Priskus laughed. "'I wish you wouldn't dooooo thaaaaaat,'" it mocked in its dizzying voice. "The orc is getting too close. He's not as dumb as you thought him."

"It's not my fault! I don't know what he found!" Selbie was utterly forlorn.

"Excuses. I know he has your amulet too. You aren't living up to your part of our deal. But that is okay," Priskus said, gliding through the table in the center of the room. "I brought an incentive."

Selbie had no chance to ask what this meant. He felt fingers lock into his hair, his head whipping back against the chair. He yelped in surprise and then felt a crude but sharp blade drag almost harmlessly against his throat. A small cut opened up on Selbie's throat, like an accidental slice from a razor.

"What...what are you doing?!" Selbie cried, squirming under the steady blade.

The shadow-being was in his face in an instant, the hideous yellow eye slowly, opening once more. "Be silent, fool."

Kenton Selbie swallowed hard, drowning the blubbering pleas that welled up in his throat. He looked away from the yellow eye, tried so hard to avoid it but everywhere his eyes pointed, the disgusting eye forced his gaze.

"Take care of the orc or I'll watch as every drop of blood in your insignificant, mortal body drains from that lying throat of yours."

"I'll take care of it," Selbie whispered. "I won't fail."

"I certainly hope you don't. You've been such a useful little man. Good help is so hard to replace."

"In the morning. I'll do it first thing in the morning. I swear it. I can come up with a plan!"

Priskus moved away from Selbie. "Good. Do it. And Selbie, if you can drive this one out, who knows, maybe I will reward you again."

The old man could only nod his head dumbly. He felt the knife move from his throat and his head flew forward from a hard shove. The shadow-form swirled into itself and then exploded silently in a dark haze. The light from the lamps lifted again, filling the room with a warm glow once more.

Selbie sat in quiet solitude, staring at nothing in particular, trying to compose himself. Instead, an idea flashed in his mind's eye, sudden and clear, and then he knew what he would do. It was so simple. A haggard smile crept across his face. This time, he couldn't fail.

CHAPTER 10

Grimluk had spent the rest of the night sleeping in fits, tossing and turning, finally waking a short time after dawn to the sound of imp wings. He rolled out of bed, sluggish at first, the echos of the imps' wings not quite fading away. He stood at the window for a few minutes after dressing, letting the new morning's light wash away the dreams. He took a deep breath and centered himself. Practiced calm slipped through him as Grimluk slipped on his boots, strapped on his gun belt, and finally slid into his coat. He felt the weight of the amulet slap against his hip and pulled it from his pocket, looking it over once again. The jewel seemed even more strange in the morning sun. The light that touched it seemed to go cold and gray. Grimluk frowned and stuffed the amulet into his bag before slinging it over his shoulder and heading downstairs. Matthew was still at the bar, waiting on his father to wake up.

"Mornin', Grimluk."

"Mornin'."

"What can I do for ya?" Matthew leaned forward. "You get food right now, it's no charge." His tone was quiet and conspiratorial.

Grimluk grinned. "If you can fry 'em up quick,

I'll take a couple of eggs and a biscuit with some water."

Matthew winked at him, quickly setting to work. He slid Grimluk a tankard of water which quickly disappeared down his gullet. He gave a nod to Matthew as the latter disappeared into the kitchen to fry up the eggs. A few minutes later, the young man returned, plopping down a tin plate.

"Appreciate it," Grimluk said.

"We need you strong. Never seen anyone punch a demon before. Lookin' forward to it!" Matthew said with a grin.

Grimluk devoured the food hastily, piling both the eggs into the biscuit. Matthew had also slipped a few slices of thick, fatty bacon onto the plate before setting out a refilled tankard. Matthew was a much better cook than his father.

With food in his belly and thanks on his lips, Grimluk slipped outside. The morning air was stiff, already hot. Grimluk slid his hat on. The afternoon heat would be unbearable. With a grunt, Grimluk stepped off the Silver Sliver's porch, ready to slip around the building and meet Ivor at the mine. He stopped as he saw two figures coming out of the Watch: Mayor Selbie and Trilgor were headed his way.

Selbie let out a sharp, "ha," upon seeing the hunter. He pointed at Grimluk, quickening his pace. Trilgor jogged along after him, a plain look of annoyance spread across his face.

Grimluk watched them approach, nodding to the young captain. He caught Selbie's eyes and nearly growled at the man. "Good morning, gentlemen."

"Good morning yourself, orc," Selbie spit out.

"Where are you running off to?"

"I was just about to meet Ivor. He thinks he might know where the demon's holed up." Even in the glaring morning sun, he could see Selbie's face go white.

"I guess it's good we caught you out here first," Trilgor replied. He hooked a thumb towards Selbie. "This one says you stole something from him under threat of violence."

"I see."

"Did you?"

"I removed something dangerous from the possession of a man who's clearly unstable," Grimluk said coldly, looking Selbie dead in the eyes.

Trilgor sighed. "I don't have any cuffs big enough for you, so please just come with me quietly."

Grimluk frowned and grunted. "Very well."

Mayor Selbie looked like he was going to burst with joy. He followed behind Trilgor and Grimluk as the former led them back to the Watch, where Trilgor reluctantly led him to a holding cell. Grimluk could hear Negos snoring away in his cell.

Before putting Grimluk inside the cell, Trilgor asked for his belongings. "Sorry," he said as he gathered everything. He motioned for Grimluk to enter the cell and then closed the door behind him, locking it. Trilgor stood back from the iron bars. Selbie watched, still aglow.

"Trilgor," Grimluk said, "We need to talk. Now."

Trilgor looked at Grimluk and then at Selbie. The mayor's face twisted into visible anger. "Captain, this man is a thief and a violent brute. Do not listen to a word he says."

"Ivor helped me figure it out, or so he thinks," Grimluk began.

"Be quiet, you wretched beast," Selbie hissed in response.

"I'm sure Charlie and Peter told you about what happened yesterday-"

"Captain, this man needs to be brought to justice. Kill him."

Trilgor whirled on the mayor, eyes wide in disbelief. "Kill him? Over theft? Have you lost your gods damned mind?! We didn't even execute Negos and he killed a man!"

Selbie ignored the comment. "I demand justice! Justice!" Trilgor began to argue but Selbie pressed on before he could speak. "Do you understand the concept of justice? Your mother did and I'm really beginning to wonder if she passed it on to you." Trilgor's face turned to stone. "Do your job, *Captain*, or I'll turn you loose back into the Wastelands. That...*thing* is dangerous," Selbie pointed at Grimluk furiously. "He's a rabid dog that needs to be put down!"

"Be silent, you whimpering old fool!" Grimluk roared from behind the bars, startling Selbie so bad he stumbled back into the wall, a hand clutched to his chest. Trilgor was caught off guard as well but let out a sigh of relief. Grimluk sneered at the old man contemptuously, letting out a growl of frustration.

"Return my property," Selbie whispered. His heart was hammering in his throat.

Trilgor acquiesced through gritted his teeth. "Fine, if it will stop you from flapping your gums anymore. What was stolen?"

"An amulet...given to me by a very dear friend," Selbie blurted out.

"Where is it, Grimluk?" Trilgor asked.

"In my bag," he said, trying to remain patient.

Trilgor opened up Grimluk's bag and dug through it. The old man acted like a spoiled child waiting on a gift. Trilgor found the amulet and pulled it out. Selbie snatched it from his hand greedily. Before he could make a speedy exit though, Trilgor grabbed the mayor by the collar and pulled him in close. "You ever mention my mother like that again and I'll break your jaw."

Selbie ripped away from Trilgor's hand, running out of the Watch with the amulet clutched to his chest. His eyes were wild and triumphant. Trilgor sneered.

Grimluk shared the sentiment, growling as the old man fled. He looked at Trilgor again. The young man met his gaze. He motioned for Grimluk to finish what he had been trying to say, listening intently as the hunter recounted the recent events of the previous day and the information he'd gathered up to then. Trilgor's face looked quite disturbed.

"Let me out of here and come with me," Grimluk finished. "We'll probably need your help anyways."

Trilgor nodded. "I'd threaten to bring more of the Watch but I know your skill. And I've seen the effect you've had on the town. I know you're true, and it's pretty damn clear that Selbie either summoned this damn thing or is under its control." He reached out and unlocked the cell, returning Grimluk's possessions.

"Good man. Now, let's go kill us a demon,"

Grimluk said.

Between the time Grimluk woke up and Kenton Selbie disappeared back to his house with the amulet reclaimed, Ivor Danshor had gathered together his own preparations for the day. Among them, a potion in an old gourd, to share between anyone entering into what might be the demon's lair, that would fortify their minds against psychic assault long enough to get the job done. It wouldn't so much protect as much as allow for endurance. Ivor also grabbed his ironwood staff. The shaft was covered in runes of a protective and warding nature. The head was home to a long crystal that shimmered like a rainbow. The old magician finished by slipping an iron dagger into his belt. Finished, Ivor headed out for the mine. He saw Grimluk and Trilgor heading his way and hailed the pair.

"I see you thought to bring the good captain along with us. Good morning, Trilgor." Ivor noticed the orcs were scowling. "What?"

"Selbie had me arrested for taking the amulet," Grimluk answered. "We need to do this quick. Are we ready to go?"

"He what? Oh, yes, we just need to get one of the miners. We might need explosives."

"We should find Orn," Trilgor remarked. "He's the best with explosives."

"Alright, then, let's get going," Ivor said.

"You two go ahead, tell Thomas I asked for Orn and then meet me at the town entrance," Trilgor said quickly. "I'm gonna grab a couple of folks for this, just in case something decides to surprise us out there."

Grimluk and Ivor headed to the mine's entrance as Trilgor ran back to the Watch. The mine itself was both in and behind the big building, which served as the bunkhouse and office. Someone was always working the desk and, under more normal circumstances, the mine was almost always active at any given hour. Thomas jumped in his chair as the pair rushed in.

"Oh, good mornin', Grimluk, Ivor, what's the rush?" Thomas asked.

"We need to see Orn, Trilgor wants him to help us," Grimluk replied. "We think we found the demon."

Thomas's face lit up. "You found it?!"

"Probably, but we need Orn, please," Ivor chimed in.

"Oh, right, yeah, hold on." Thomas disappeared up the stairs, his feet thumping against the steps. Overhead, they could hear him running down the hallway and then frantically knocking on a door. Thomas quickly explained the situation to Orn. The dwarf sprang into motion, sliding into his boots and snatching the keys to the equipment room off a hook near the door. Thomas led the way back down the stairs, with Orn close behind.

"Here he is!" Thomas exclaimed.

"Yeah, I'm here. Thomas says you found the demon and Trilgor asked for me. What's going on?"

"I think the demon's nested in the original mine. Grimluk here had a run-in with it and managed to use the attack to get a peek at its location. No one would've even known that's what it was but my master had helped start the original mine excavation and wrote down what happened. It all sounded the same as what Grimluk saw. They collapsed the entrance and moved down here and now here we are. Trilgor said you were best with explosives."

Orn stood there dumbstruck. "I, uh, guess so. Shit...I guess that's why you never got over here to talk to us."

"That's right," Grimluk replied. "Trilgor said he'd meet us at the barrier. Get what you need and let's go. The sooner we get this over with, the sooner your town gets back to what passes for normal out here in the Wastelands."

"Easy, hunter, I understand. Spare a moment and we can go," Orn said. He disappeared through a door at the back of the building that led into the mine itself and, more specifically, the equipment room. Orn grabbed a supply of explosives. Several big sticks bound together and a batch of smaller, individual sticks that he stuffed into a bag with fuses. For good measure, he grabbed a pair of lanterns as well. Moments later, he rejoined the others.

Grimluk nodded. "Let's get out there."

Thomas stopped them first. "Good luck, fellas."

"Thank you, Thomas," Grimluk said. "If we succeed, come to the Sliver later and I'll buy you a drink and tell you what happened."

"Well, far be it from me to turn down a free drink. You're legally obligated to kill that fucker now." Thomas said, trying to act as if the free drink was a nuisance.

Grimluk grinned.

Trilgor raced into the bunkhouse and immediately spotted Peter and Charlie. "Good news, you two. Selbie's an asshole and Ivor thinks he knows where the demon is. Guess who gets to come help."

"Gods damn it, Cap, I'm not even on duty today," Peter protested.

"I know, I know, I promise I'll give you a whole month off duty after this," Trilgor said in attempt to reassure the man. "And you too, Char."

Peter sighed and grabbed his rifle. Charlie shrugged and did the same. "So what's the situation?" she asked.

Trilgor gave them the rundown of what they were doing as he led them to the barrier. Peter gulped, touching his bruised cheek tenderly. The whole ordeal scared him but the thought that they could be free of the thing did more to ease his spirits than his captain's offer of free time.

The three Watchmen stood in wait for only a short time. Grimluk, Ivor, and Orn arrived swiftly.

"Great, everyone's here," Trilgor proclaimed.

"Which way do we go, Ivor?" Grimluk asked.

"Well, we head left obviously but I'm not sure how far. We should see the rubble pretty easily though."

Trilgor told the two Watchmen on duty to keep a sharp eye out. The energy sizzled as the posse passed through it to begin their trek. The midmorning sun beat down on them as they walked, the air still, seemingly refusing to help relieve the growing heat.

"Here," Ivor began, "everyone take a drink of this." He untied the gourd on his belt. "I cooked this up last night and it occurs to me, we already need it. This potion will fortify our minds. We'll be able to better withstand any attack this thing throws at us. By the time we find the cave, it should be active. And if it's in there, it probably already knows we're coming."

Ivor downed some of the concoction and passed it on to Orn, who remarked at how salty it was. Then Charlie, who found it bitter. Peter tasted nothing. Trilgor turned the gourd up, surprised at how sweet it tasted before passing it at last to Grimluk, who made no comment on the taste.

It wasn't long before those not usually experienced in magic began to feel the effects. Their minds seemed to become sharper, their steps lighter. They felt ready. Peter even managed to stop looking worried for a few minutes.

"Old man, remind me to get you in Mattias's distillery when we get back home," Charlie remarked. "You make a mighty fine drink."

Ivor just shook his head with a wry grin.

A short while later, the rubble finally came into view, sticking out easily against the uniform lines of the bluffs. Grimluk sped up, leading the way for the posse. After looking at the rubble, he called for Orn.

Orn approached the pile, inspecting the sealed hole with rough fingers. After a moment or two, he settled on the left side and removed a few bigger rocks. He pulled one of the smaller explosives from his bag, along with the bundle of fuses, and a box of matches from his pocket.

"This is gonna be loud. Ya might want to turn around too," Orn advised as he set the fuse to the stick. He lit the match and the fuse sparked to life, flickering and hissing. Orn dropped the stick into the crevice he'd made and quickly joined the others. Everyone did as he'd said and turned their backs, covered their ears, and lowered their heads.

A crack-boom went off behind them and a rush of air slapped their backs. Orn looked back as pebbles rained down on them and smiled at his handy work. The tunnel was mostly clear, with a few head-sized rocks rolling back into the dark as dust swirled about. Everyone readied a weapon as they entered. Ivor stamped his staff down once and commanded, "light." The crystal on his staff lit up, illuminating the old chamber in a strong but pale, yellow glow. Orn lit the lanterns and handed one to Trilgor.

The tunnel's ceiling began to get lower as they went on, enough that Grimluk and Trilgor had to duck down some. Grimluk pressed a hand to the roof to keep himself properly oriented as he walked. Each step echoed down the long passage. Occasionally, rock chips fell from the roof as Grimluk's hand ran over it. For a moment, he thought he heard a small screech up ahead. As they walked on, he heard it again.

"Anyone else hear the screeches?" Grimluk asked.

They all had. The closer they got, the more strangeness they heard until finally, a few dozen yards into the tunnel, they finally stepped into a large chamber.

The cave was exactly as Grimluk had described it. Directly on the other side of the chamber, sat a dais with huge slab of stone, carved with various symbols. They approached, shining light on the altar. Behind it stood the statue he'd seen, now in full view. The thing's legs appeared lupine and six arms spread out on either side of its slender body in front of the huge bat wings. Spiraling horns sprouted from a grotesque head whose mouth gaped in a frozen roar. Four eyes surrounded one large, central eye. All five eyes glowed with malice.

Grimluk stared up at the statue, boring back into the malevolent eyes, his revolver at the ready, arm poised to snap to point at a moment's notice. Charlie and Peter stayed in back, watching the group's rear. Ivor walked up the dais, inspecting the stone altar while Trilgor stood silently next to Orn, giving a whistle of disbelief.

"What do you think, old man?" Grimluk asked the magician.

"I think...I think it wasn't shitting you with its name. This thing is old. A few centuries at least."

"Charlie, if you don't get the fuck out of my ear," Peter said suddenly, his voice raising. He turned a look of annoyance at his partner. Charlie opened her mouth to respond but Peter's sudden look of realization stopped him short of finishing his thought. "Oh. It's not you. It's...talking to me."

Slowly, each of them began to grow aware of the demon's whispers as well. The words were weak, but the longer they stood there, the clearer they became. It mocked them each, privately, directly into their minds, telling them how they would die, how it would feast on their agony, torture their souls.

Peter heard the thing talk about murdering his family. How it would disembowel Cassie, slowly, and then drown her in her own blood. How it would choke Nicholas to death on the woman's guts while

Gwen watched. Priskus threatened pain for he and his family. Physical and spiritual.

Charlie kept hearing different ways she could and would die. It whispered to her that one day, she'd break up a fight and get her head blown off by a drunk. Or that she'd wake up covered in vipers. It taunted her, calling her a coward, telling her in the end, she'd swing from a rope or jam a pistol barrel in her own mouth.

Trilgor was taunted with the death of all the people under his charge and the death of everyone under his protection. The voice told him that it would string him up while the town burned, no one able to escape. It told him about marauders that would arrive and slaughter everyone, leaving him alive to wallow in his failure. He would never be allowed to die before witnessing those losses.

Orn stood with a look of utter confusion on his face, hearing a strange mix of words from the demon. It promised agony and death but also gave thanks to his people for their "help." That, Priskus said, would ensure Orn's death would be swift and his soul devoured quickly. Even still, it described every ounce of suffering that awaited him.

Ivor stood on the dais with a scowl on his face. All the old magician could make out was the occasional mention of his soul. Grimluk was concentrating, trying to understand what he heard. He realized Priskus wasn't speaking to him, so much as trying to vent its fury straight into his mind. In unison, his eyes and gun snapped towards the roof of the cave. A lone screech hit their ears followed by the sound of talons on stone echoing from above.

"They're coming." Grimluk cocked the hammer.

The Watchmen trained their rifles overhead, their captain following with his pistol. They all stood, watching, waiting on the creatures to show themselves. Tension coiled around them while Priskus worked to break through their fortified minds. Another screech hit their ears from the ceiling. Grimluk's brows furrowed. A tiny body glided to the cavern floor in front of him. An imp.

The thing clawed uselessly at Grimluk's boot, lacking the strength to even scuff it. Several more came tumbling down. One landed on Orn, who plucked it off of his head and, with a look of horror, hurled the creature at one of its brethren. The pair collided and rolled off into the dark. The rest were either kicked away or their wings folded and they crashed. Grimluk stooped down and eyed the imp at his feet. Its yellow eyes looked up into his and the two stared at each other. The imp knew it was too weak to attack but sheer spite kept it from giving up the prospect of aggression.

Grimluk let out a lone laugh. Another followed and then he stood up, apparently giddy and giggling. The others looked at him like his mind was gone. Charlie wanted to throw her rifle up at him, fearing he'd finally snapped but stayed her hand. All of them looked at each other in confusion as Grimluk's mighty frame began shaking with laughter.

"I think our demon hunter's had it," Peter said bleakly to Charlie.

Ivor just watched the hunter, slightly amused. "I never seen an orc laugh so hard before."

The laughter boomed out of Grimluk in great peals of belly laughter. As he began to settle down, he slid the huge revolver back into its holster. "Priskus, you shitheel, I know what you are," he said more to himself than the demon. He looked at the others again, choking down the aftershocks of his laughter. "It's fear!" Grimluk exclaimed. "It feeds on fear. All of its power lies in fear. Without its secrecy, without the unknown, without challenging it outright, without dragging our fears out into the light, it can't wreak havoc. Just like it did to you all."

"That would certainly explain a lot," Ivor responded. "And why the potions are working so well. It used up a lot of energy on you yesterday."

Waves of relief washed over the group. Charlie collapsed to her butt. One by one, they all began to laugh. A very dull roar cut their heads, all of its edge lost now. Grimluk suggested they further strip Priskus of its power by sharing their fears once more, as many of the townsfolk had already done with him, and set loose the burdens it tried to force on them.

Each person spoke, voices trembling at first at exposing themselves but each word pushed the demon's influence farther away until they could no longer hear it. Orn shared that the mention of his people "helping" scared the shit out of him more than death. Charlie had nearly fell apart in sobs at the mention of suicide. Peter helped his friend up and squeezed her hand. Charlie smiled and clasped Peter's shoulder.

"Thanks," she said, wiping away tears.

Trilgor shared his own fears before telling Charlie and Peter how proud of them he was. Ivor confessed, almost apologetically, that he didn't fear failure or death and had no one to lose but that he could feel Priskus trying to gnaw at his fear of the things he'd seen in the Wastelands.

Grimluk smiled. "Well, I'd say it's time to finish up and get ourselves out of here. Orn, can you take this shit down? That oughta flush its ass out so I can end this."

Orn nodded and fished the other explosives, the big bundle this time, and more fuses out of his bag. He whistled a tune to himself as he plugged the bundle with fuses. He looked up at the statue's unsettling face and then motioned for Grimluk.

"I need your help for this one. I think you'll enjoy the task."

Grimluk walked over to the old miner. Orn handed up a lone stick with a fresh fuse.

"Stick this fucker in the mouth," Orn said pointing up at the statue's gaping maw. "Hard to talk without a head, ain't it?"

Grimluk grinned as he took the explosive. The statue's eyes were glowing brighter and the whole thing shook with the slightest of tremors. Orn set the bundle of explosives down at his feet, between the altar and the statue. He and Grimluk each struck a match and lit their respective fuses. As soon as the sparks began to go, all six of them took off for the outside world once more. Once in the tunnel, the explosions boomed behind them, blowing a cloud of dust after them. Celebration was cut short though as a hideous shriek filled the tunnel, drowning out the echoes of the blast. A hard rush of air burst through them, cold as the grave. The posse spilled back out into the sunlight, blinding themselves for a moment in the transition. Ears ringing and eyes adjusting to the light again, they stood silently, resting.

"Once we get back to town, I can summon

Priskus to a bird or something and then kill it. Let's get going," Grimluk said. The others followed quickly behind.

Halfway back to town, Trilgor approached him. "So...you can put this asshole in a chicken or something?"

A lone laugh escaped Grimluk's lips. "Wouldn't be the first time. Have you ever seen a chicken filled with a manifestation of evil?"

Trilgor shook his head. "Can't say I have."

"It's an evil most fowl."

From behind them, Peter and Charlie groaned and booed at him. "Hey, you in the front, fuck you!" Charlie teased. Ivor rolled his eyes and chuckled. Orn looked confused for a moment but then it clicked and he started laughing. Their merriment was short-lived, however. Gun shots rang out from the town, echoing across the valley.

CHAPTER 11

Kenton Selbie sat alone behind his big desk nursing a bottle of brandy. An old shotgun sat out in front of him next to a box of shells that hadn't been opened in some time. Selbie mumbled to himself in between drinks, trying to work up the courage to get back into the Watch and kill Grimluk. So far, he'd only managed to give himself a headache. He took a swig of the brandy and reached up, idly touching the arcane piece of jewelry once more dangling from his neck.

Sudden panic ripped through his mind with life or death urgency. The feeling came upon him so suddenly he couldn't help but let out a cry. Selbie sat bolt upright as he heard Priskus scream his name in a garbled, distorted shriek.

"THE ORC!" it bellowed.

"What?! I'm going to kill him! I am! Look at the gun! I'll do it, damn it!" Selbie wailed. The panic was threatening to rip his nerves out.

"Found my...."

"What?!" Selbie shouted.

"They found my altar!" it hissed into his mind. Priskus began trying to manifest in front of the old man but all it could manage was a vague shadow that filled the room.

Selbie's heart dropped as realization dawned on him. He wanted to ask what to do, what was going on but the words clung to his tongue. The shadow faded for a moment but then seemed to grow darker again.

"Protect me, you fool. If the orc ends me, you die." The demon's words echoed through Selbie's mind. Priskus felt the old man's fear and clung to it like a raft in a storm.

Selbie mindlessly drank more of the brandy as he rose from his chair. He stuffed a handful of shotgun shells into his vest pocket and then breached the gun, slipping two fresh shells into each barrel and snapped it shut. The steel of the barrel focused his mind. Selbie touched the amulet. Fear filled him but now anger began to rise. He would not let the green-skinned savage fuck up everything he'd been working towards. Selbie dashed down the stairs and out of the house with wild eyes. He marched towards the center of town. Jhaan and another woman, her friend, Nthanda, had just walked out of the store, chatting as Nthanda left. Selbie lifted the shotgun and both barrels exploded. Screams erupted as the lead tore through them. Jhaan and Nthanda lay twitching as the life rapidly drained from them. Blackness began to swell up around them as they died. For one, brief moment, there was nothing and nothingness, eternity stretching out before each woman, alone despite dying together.

But the moment past and light exploded in the darkness. Kenton Selbie's voice rang out.

Wesson came barreling out of his shop in time to see Jhaan and Nthanda resurrect. The smith looked at the women rising to their feet in a wholly unnatural manner and Selbie holding the smoking scattergun. Wesson charged towards the mayor like a bull. Before he could get within three feet of the man though, Selbie shouted, "stop!" Jhaan jerked out and slammed a thin arm into Wesson's throat. The man's feet flew out in front of him and he landed on his neck with a sick snap. Moments later, Selbie walked up, closing the breach with fresh shells loaded. Wesson felt heat for a fraction of a second and then blackness took him for a moment as well.

Selbie shouted for Wesson to get to his feet. The amulet flashed its eerie light and Wesson's skull began to reform, his body lurching up the same way the women's had moments before. All three of them were whole again. All three of their faces were masks of anguish, tears streaming as Selbie commanded them.

Selbie made his way towards the town's entrance, his new charges ahead of him, ready to meet Grimluk and end him. A pair of Watchmen rushed at him but the trio of corpses took them down with little trouble, leaving them in an unconscious heap. The Watchmen at the town's entrance had turned at the commotion and saw their comrades crumpled in a heap.

"Stop where you are!" one of the Watchmen shouted. The women both had their rifles aimed at the quartet.

Selbie laughed. "Why don't you be good little minions and get the fuck out of my way."

"I said stop!" she shouted again.

The group kept coming towards them. The Watchmen opened fire, bullets ripping into Selbie's new meat shields. The duo watched in horror as the trio kept coming. A volley of rifle fire only served to waste ammo. Jhaan and Nthanda rushed them and knocked the pair aside from the barrier's edge. Grimluk and the others arrived in time to see the Watchmen fall.

"Selbie!" Grimluk roared.

"The fuck are you doing, old man?" Trilgor shouted.

"Why couldn't you keep that piece of shit in the cell, Trilgor," Selbie shouted. "This is on your hands. You fucking orcs! You two, I want this ended. Kill them."

Jhaan and Nthanda attempted to run through the barrier but it knocked them away, crackling and snapping, burning their undead flesh. They tried again and again as Selbie growled in growing frustration, finally pointing his shotgun at Grimluk. Before he could fire, a yelp escaped his lips as his leg came out from under him. One of the fallen Watchmen, the woman who'd shouted for them to stop, had kicked at the back of his knee. The shotgun fired into the sky with both barrels. Nthanda pounced and left the Watchman dazed.

"What's the matter, Mr. Mayor," Grimluk chided, "I thought you were ending this."

"There's more than one way to kill you," Selbie called. The amulet flashed again. By now, more Watchmen had gathered around. The old man turned around quickly, Wesson moving in front of him to block the gun barrels currently pointed his way. Jhaan and Nthanda rushed the Watchmen in a mad dash, fighting jaggedly but with brutal effectiveness, breaking or dislocating bones. Selbie ran off back towards the safety of his house, Wesson following behind as his shield.

"After him!" Trilgor shouted. "Ivor, check on the wounded!"

"I got it," the old magician said, going to work.

Grimluk took off in a dead sprint after Selbie, trailing behind Nthanda and Jhaan as they tried to catch up to Selbie. His revolver slid out, firing twice as he ran. The first shot took out Nthanda's leg, bringing the woman down in a hard roll. The second shot exploded the dirt ahead and to Selbie's left, spraying rough clumps of earth. Nthanda was on her feet again and all four of them quickly slipped through Selbie's front gate with Wesson and Selbie disappearing inside. Trilgor, Orn, Charlie, and Peter caught up with Grimluk.

"What now?" Trilgor asked.

"They're like Ald'n. Which means the only thing that can stop them is Selbie telling them to stop. Or removing the amulet," Grimluk replied. He worked his jaw in thought. "I think."

"We can figure it out. He's not going anywhere, can't go anywhere, and I'd bet our pal Priskus has latched on to him," Trilgor said. "And you seemed to handle Ald'n pretty damn well. I think between the two of us, we can get through them and get to Selbie."

"Cap'n," Peter interrupted, nodding towards the woman coming their way. Trilgor turned. It was the other woman who'd been on gate duty.

"Sir," she said, her eyes wide with fear, speaking as calmly as she could. "We got more trouble."

"What the fuck else is going on now?" Trilgor spat.

"Well...uh...it's the graveyard. It's, uh, it's waking up."

Ivor looked at Grimluk. "I think it's safe to say that amulet is more powerful than I thought. And those definitely *aren't* ghouls. Normally, I give the dead a little something to keep them from turning but this..." The magician's seemed to age as worry fell over him, making him look ready to lay down into the dust.

Grimluk growled. He looked out at Selbie's house again. Jhaan and Nthanda stood still as stone in the small yard, silent guardians who weren't supposed to be there. "Will the barrier hold?"

"It damn well ought to. Things worse than walking corpses have bounced off it." Ivor seemed almost insulted that Grimluk had even asked such a question.

"All the same, be prepared," Grimluk began. "Trilgor, go keep watch. I think the best way to handle the corpses is dismemberment. Don't waste your ammo. If the barrier can't hold them, your Watchmen will be the only defense. I'll go take care of Selbie."

"You sure you can handle all that alone?" Trilgor asked.

"I've handled worse. Luck be with us, though."

Trilgor turned around as another Watchman ran up to report the denizens of the Greenreach Bluffs graveyard were now at the barrier. The young captain led his charges, along with Ivor and Orn, back to the front of the town. The rest of the Watchmen had already set up a perimeter just in case. They all stood aghast, looking out at some of the poor souls already there.

By the time each of the dead had made it to

town, they were mostly whole again and banging away at the barrier, flinging themselves into it with savage abandon. Their faces told another story. Faces were scrawled with frustration and sadness. Their eyes glistened with tears as they tried to fight the outside will controlling them, not understanding what compelled the violence or their return to life. Peter wanted to scream at the sight of a crying skeleton, still knitting itself back together as it shambled into the barrier. The dead's sobs filled the Watchmen's ears.

The barrier repelled the undead attackers though, each body causing the mystical energies to sizzle and crackle. Every time a limb made contact, it would begin decaying again. Selbie's mysterious amulet was quite powerful indeed, and almost immediately the decay would halt and reverse once more. Even still, each blow hurt them. No matter how quickly it passed, it was still excruciating.

Still they came. The cacophony of pain had attracted the attention of the rest of the town finally. People started filing out to see what was going on. The farmers rushed up to Trilgor, frantically asking what on Arkod was going on. He began to explain but then something caught his eyes.

His mother had appeared, taking up rank in the assault. Trilgor staggered towards her. "Mom?"

"Hello-" she brought down both fists into the barrier and cried out as it knocked her away, "son. Am I-" another blow, "a vampire? Did that thing turn me?"

Trilgor's legs nearly gave out. "No, mom. It'd...it'd take too long to explain. You're not a vampire, but you are-" his jaw clenched.

"What?" she said, hurling herself at the barrier again. "What is it?"

"Mom, you're still dead. Or supposed to be. All of you are."

She said nothing.

The townsfolk had gathered behind the Watchmen as Trilgor and his mother spoke. Fear found root in them once more. Fear shook them as they watched their loved ones, awake from what should have been an unending slumber. Priskus felt the fear rise and attempted to feed on it. The demon was too weak to get very much though. The barrier still kept him from feeding properly and without an anchor to the mortal world, Priskus was stuck trying to hold to Selbie or else be flung back to the Abyss once more. The demon, for the first time in its millennial-long existence, felt a twinge of the fear it had inflicted on so many. Then, an idea came to it. It took one last gulp of the rising terror in the town and then reached out.

Grimluk walked silently toward Selbie's house. Jhaan and Nthanda stood in the courtyard, watching him. Sadness filled their eyes. He looked at them from outside the gate, feeling pity for them and for what was now transpiring.

"I'm sorry this happened to you," he called out to them.

"You tried," Jhaan said, her jaw tight.

"I'll stop him. I'll end this. I promise." He looked them each in the eyes and repeated himself. "I promise."

Smoothly, deliberately, Grimluk opened the gate

and stepped into his battleground. Both women, faces contorted in desperation, bodies jerking as they tried with all their power to resist, dove at him like starving cougars. He plowed through them, throwing out arms like oak limbs. Collarbones snapped on impact and the force knocked them away. Jhaan and Nthanda immediately hit their feet again, bones resetting as they stood, bodies tensed as they continued trying to resist Selbie's control.

Grimluk knew what their bodies were capable of after his fight with Ald'n. This time, instead of trying to kill the brain, he would try a new plan. Nthanda lurched forward, swinging both hands at Grimluk's face, clawing for his throat. He dodged, her hands passing through air. With all his speed, he stepped forward again, driving his skull into his attacker's nose. Nthanda stumbled back, momentarily stunned. Jhaan leaped at him, slamming into his massive frame. He took the blow and grabbed her arm. With a jerk, Grimluk spun, flinging Jhaan into Nthanda. The women tumbled away into a heap.

The pair untangled from each other, practically slithering away. Jhaan leaped into the air, bounding over Grimluk. The move distracted him long enough for Nthanda to rush him, hammering his chest with quick blows. Jhaan attacked him from the rear, striking for his kidneys. A grunt of pain slipped out of his mouth. A mule-kick pushed Jhaan away. Grimluk swung at Nthanda with a left, then filled her gut with a powerful right, doubling her over.

Grimluk took Nthanda and hurled her one handed into the low stone wall surrounding the courtyard. The loud snap from the impact echoed out. No sooner had he let her go than Jhaan leaped on his back, clawing wildly at his face, drawing several long gashes across his cheek. Grimluk threw a haphazard fist at her face that connected enough to dislodge her. He stepped away, towards the house, bleeding and trying to plan his attack. He had an idea.

The women rushed in again. Jhaan stepped into a haymaker that sent her spinning. Grimluk kneed Nthanda and then pulled her head-first into the stone steps leading to the front door, smashing her skull. He spun quickly, blocking savage clawing from Jhaan. A tree-trunk knee doubled her over. Grimluk hefted her lithe body up at her gut, lifting her to his shoulder and then slammed her down onto the heavy iron gate, impaling Jhaan through her lower back. She hung unevenly, thrashing about.

Nthanda had risen again when he turned around and came running at him, screaming. Grimluk threw his left hand out, catching her by the throat, then with his right, drew his revolver. He turned, dragging her along, and in one fluid motion filled with brutal strength, threw Nthanda into the air, up and over Jhaan. The huge revolver went up and fired, filling the air with the sound of a small cannon.

The bullet ripped through Nthanda's throat, removing most of her head from her body, spraying blood and bone everywhere. The body landed hard.

Jhaan screamed at Grimluk, trying to lift herself off the gate, feet trying to find some sort of leverage. There was none. She tried to kick the hunter to no avail. Grimluk looked back at the heavy door that led into Selbie's house. It remained closed. He trained the barrel at the knob and fired off a new shot. The door frame splintered, taking the catch with it.

Kenton Selbie's heart tried to leap through his

chest at the sounds of gunfire. In his fear, he poured aggression into his charges. Every dead thing under his control suddenly roared with rage. They were then overpowered beyond all reason, no longer even able to exert any effort to the illusion they still had their own will. The jerky motions stopped. The horde growing at the town's entrance crashed upon the barrier like a flood breaking against a wall. Wesson filled the open doorway. Someone moved to join him.

"Aw, fuck," Grimluk said.

Ald'n stood next to Wesson.

CHAPTER 12

Nicholas sat bolt upright in his bed. He could hear the growing chorus at the town's edge. As the boy stood up from the bed, his sister looked over at him. Gwen's eyes were black.

"Go, boy, and do what you're meant to do," the voice said. Gwen's gaze followed Nicholas as he slipped out the bedroom door.

Cassie paced anxiously in the front room, trying to ignore the sounds that had begun to spill in from outside. Her brow was wrinkled from worry, waiting for Peter to return. Nicholas watched for a moment. When her back was turned, he made for the front door. Cassie turned in time to see her son running out of the apartment, jumping as the door slammed into the wall.

"Nicholas!" she cried, rushing after him.

The boy practically flew down the stairs, racing out into the dusty street and off towards the temple. Cassie watched from the balcony, ready to burst into tears, as Nicholas ran past Selbie's gate, and Grimluk's continuing fight with the two dead women. She ran back into the house for Gwen, nearly bowling her daughter over.

"Momma, where's brother going?" Gwen asked.

"I don't know, sweetie, but I need to go get him. Stay in your room, it's dangerous out."

"No no no, momma, take me with you! I'm scared." Gwen's lip trembled.

Cassie sighed. She couldn't leave Gwen alone and scared. If something happened, she'd never forgive herself. She scooped her daughter up, both of them jumping at the sound of gunfire before Cassie chased after her son, pressing Gwen's head into her shoulder. She ran as fast as she could, passing Nthanda's body, nearly screaming at another thunderclap from Grimluk's gun as he fired on Selbie's door. She felt her heart beating in her chest.

Gwen's heart was pounding as well and she lifted her head up enough from her mother's shoulder to see what had caused her to run harder. A tiny gasp escaped from her mouth at the sight of Nthanda's writhing, headless body. She'd seen visions from the spirit in her but seeing a real corpse, and a living one at that, was different. She buried her head back against her mother's shoulder and shut her eyes tight.

Cassie ran headlong into the silence and dim light of Ivor's temple, still confused and very worried about her son, her eyes quickly attempting to adjust to the change in light. She stepped slowly into the main chamber, looking for Nicholas. Something moved to her right. The momentarily darkened form of her son appearing from out of a side tunnel.

"Nicholas!" Cassie cried out. "What are you doing, honey, it's dangerous out, we have to stay inside until your father gets back." The words came spilling out. She set Gwen down and rushed to her son. She stopped short though, noticing the large crystal he was carrying. It was bigger than the boy's head and shimmered like a rainbow made of glass. "What is that? What are you doing? We have to get back home, it's not safe, come on, put that down." Cassie reached out for the crystal but Nicholas jumped back, giving her an icy stare. "Nicky, we gotta go," she said urgently.

Nicholas stared into his mother's eyes. He seemed frozen, transfixed where he stood. He didn't blink, he barely seemed to breathe. Cassie reached for him again, more insistent this time, and grabbed his arm. Nicholas ripped free from her hand.

"No, Mother, this is where I need to be." He lifted the crystal over his head and brought it down with a sharp yell and all the strength he could muster.

The crystal cracked as it hit the floor, a chunk of it sliding off somewhere into the chamber. For a moment, Cassie, Gwen, and Nicholas stared at the crystal. It cracked again, loudly, like ice breaking from a sudden shift in temperature. Cracks splintered out all over until the colors surged violently, energy rippling in small arcs over the surface before it fell apart, shattering into thousands of tiny shards. The colors disappeared, leaving each fragment gray.

"What was that, Nicholas, what did you do?!" Cassie shouted.

"What I was asked to do," Nicholas replied matter-of-factly, staring into his mother's horrified face. There was a loud snap from outside, like a lightning bolt had struck the town. "And there's one thing left."

Before Cassie could ask what was left, Nicholas struck with a viper's quickness. She looked down at Nicholas's hand and the knife held within it. He twisted the blade.

"Good-bye, mother." Nicholas's voice was ice. He struck again and again, creating fresh new wounds that blossomed with thick, red blood, coating his hand in gore. He buried his face in the blood, letting it cascade down his neck, sticky and hot. Cassie began to collapse onto her son but he stepped aside, letting her hit the stone floor with hard thud. She vainly pressed her hands to her stomach.

Cassie's eyes filled with tears, consumed with shock and sorrow. Nicholas rolled her over and sat on her chest, his face still, eyes wide. "Why?" she asked, more mouthing the word than speaking it.

"Because I needed a sacrifice," he muttered before pounding the knife into her chest. He opened a hole big enough to fit his hand inside, grabbing onto his mother's still beating heart. "Pure fear and pure blood from the heart." Cassie screamed.

A wave of darkness rolled over mother and son. Nicholas's eyes glowed red as Priskus's spirit latched onto the boy's body. As Cassie began to lose consciousness, she tried to stroke Nicholas's blood-covered cheek. Something that was and was not her son looked down at her, slapping her hand away. Nicholas pulled his hand out of his mother's chest and turned around. Gwen was gone.

****

A dozen corpses threw themselves at the barrier once more only to hit the ground or stumble forward as the barrier dispersed. The dead scrambled to their feet in a mad rage, slamming into the line of Watchmen like a tidal wave. Many of the corpses cried out, still trying to resist the power that controlled their bodies. In they flooded all the same.

Ivor turned as the violent torrent swarmed in and ran. Not in fear of the dead but for fear of why the barrier dropped. Either Selbie had slipped by Grimluk or someone else was helping the good mayor. So he ran back to the temple as the Watchmen fought back the horde.

Without a word from their captain, several Watchmen sounded an alarm to warn the citizens of the city while their comrades began hacking away with any blade they could get. Men and women with sabers and axes cleaved the limbs off friends and relatives. A few foolhardy citizens ran up with shovels, in their effort to keep their town safe.

The corpses kept coming.

Over the cacophony of screams and metal meeting meat, the ground split with small fissures, letting loose the dulled but powerful sound of a roar. The ground shook all around. The long dead lake bed splintered and cracked, dry earth heaving as a long dead creature rose to life once more. The raging corpses halted, Selbie's concentration clearly faltering at the sound of the roar.

A few dozen yards from the town's border, long, black horns broke through the surface of the desert. The dirt and rock burst away in a shower as the dragon's snout opened. It roared at the sky, a millennia old rage bellowing from the creature's regenerating throat. Talons gripped the top soil and worked to pull their owner free of its tomb. Wads of black phlegm shot out of the beast's throat as it hacked and wheezed in between roars. Choked fire lit up in staccato bursts.

The dragon's back legs tightened, ancient muscles coiling. The beast shot out of its grave and into the air. Wings spread out, as the creature attempted to take flight once more but the flesh hadn't yet reformed. It crashed, sliding to a stop in front of a stunned crowd of living and dead alike. The dragon's red eyes glared out, its mind focused on assaulting anything in its path, moving with a will not entirely its own. Unlike the dead villagers, however, the dead dragon didn't care. It wanted carnage. It wanted to crush bones, rend flesh, and burn the world.

****

Grimluk barreled at Wesson and Ald'n, firing once at each of them. The first shot ripped through Wesson's thigh, staggering him. The second ripped a hole open in Ald'n's chest, causing him to stumble back. Grimluk fired at Wesson again, putting a hole in his shoulder and loosing a left hook into the smith's face a moment later. Wesson spun around, a lone tooth flying out of his mouth, and slammed into Ald'n. They fell hard in a pile. Now in the house, he holstered his gun, one bullet left.

His opponents rose, staring down at him. Grimluk stared back. Wesson stepped forward, throwing a wild punch with his right hand. Ald'n spun around the smith, throwing a quick left. Grimluk did his best to block both blows but Ald'n's speed was still just as great as before and the elf landed his blow. The momentary daze was the opening they needed and the two began to hammer the hunter mercilessly.

Grimluk staggered with a hard grunt, spinning into the busted door as Ald'n decked him again. He responded with a savage mule kick that sent the elf sprawling. Wesson's heavy fist bounced off of Grimluk's shoulder. He threw his elbow backwards into the man's temple, pushing him away.

The sound of the barrier falling rang out, distracting Grimluk. Wesson stepped in for another punch but froze a moment later as the dragon bellowed. Grimluk felt ice fill his blood. He noticed Wesson and Ald'n had frozen at the sounds of the dragon and decided to use the opportunity to his advantage, pulling his knife. Grimluk grabbed a handful of Wesson's hair and swung the knife as hard as he could. The blade, incredibly honed, sliced through skin and muscle easily and slid through bone with pure, brute force. Grimluk kicked the headless body into the still-frozen Ald'n before hurling the head out the front door.

Grimluk heard Selbie cry out at the sound of the impact and Ald'n went into a rage once more as the old man regained his concentration with the dead. The elf slammed into him, taking him down hard, throwing wild punches. Grimluk grabbed the back of Ald'n's head and brought him down, meeting the elf's nose with his forehead. The blow dazed Ald'n for a moment, giving Grimluk time to slash at the dead man's eyes with the knife. He dumped his flailing attacker off and then put the prone elf face down to the floor. The big knife went through the elf's back, pinning him through the shoulder blades. Grimluk grabbed both the man's thrashing arms at the elbow, planting a boot square in the small of his back and pulled with a roar. A chorus of pops, wet cracks, and tearing filled the room as Grimluk ripped the elf's arms free.

Behind him, Wesson's body swung wildly, knocking over furniture. Below him, Ald'n thrashed and screamed. When the dragon roared again, Grimluk barreled up the stairs as quickly as he could, panting, covered in sweat and blood. Selbie's office door stood open. The old man stood stock still in front of his big desk, breathing quickly and shaking. Sadie stood in front of him with a gun to her head.

"Stop there, orc!" Selbie shouted.

****

As Ivor ran back to the temple, he saw Gwen come running out, racing past him. He called out, telling her to go hide, but she kept running. He frowned but returned his focus to the crystal. He had to get the barrier back up. The Watchmen would never stop all the attackers, nevermind that a dragon had arrived moments after he'd taken off. He tried to ignore the second roar.

"Of course there's a fucking dragon now," Ivor muttered angrily to himself. He kept moving as quick as his knees would take him. As he passed under the archway and into the shifting light, he didn't have time to avoid running into the boy. They collided but only Ivor went down.

"What-" Ivor began to ask but stopped when he saw the blood covering Nicholas's face. "Are you alright, boy?"

Without a word, Nicholas flicked his hand and Ivor was slung back into the temple, slamming through a table and sliding under another. Dazed, he crawled out from under the table and began limping towards the crystal's chamber. Ivor groaned when he saw Cassie's body, his stomach tumbling at all the blood surrounding her. He walked over to her and knelt. She wasn't healing or attacking him, so she wasn't dead. Yet. He managed to pry his eyes away and saw the crystal shards at her feet.

"Shit!" he hissed. Cassie began to stir with life once more, catching his attention again. "I'm sorry, Mrs. Quinn. I don't have time to deal with you." He planted his staff next to her and began chanting, almost singing. Seconds later, the stone under Cassie began to turn soft. Her body sank into the rock, dropping down enough that Ivor was assured freedom from attack while he worked. Unfortunately, he was not assured freedom from the cries of sadness and rage that poured out of her. He scooped up the biggest of the shards and walked away with a heavy heart to focus on his task.

****

Any training and plan Trilgor had given the Watchmen died the moment the dragon appeared. Up until then, they'd relied on the barrier and never thought of what would happen if something truly bad showed up in its absence. Now both were happening at the same time. Trilgor attempted to lead a charge, beheading or dismembering as many of the distracted dead as he could get to, except for his mother, who watched him as he sent a headless body flying. She saw the dragon focus on her son.

As it spit out a wad of the tar at Trilgor, his mother shoved him out of the way. The black phlegm slammed into and enveloped her, holding her fast. The creature rose, standing tall over the crowd, still regenerating but proving it was no less of a threat. It leaped forward, razor-sharp talons ripped through flesh and bone of dead and living alike. Terrified townsfolk who had tried to help the Watchmen were punished for their folly. The dragon, still trying to summon its flames, hurled more wads of the sticky, black phlegm indiscriminately. The stuff dried quickly, hardening and trapping anyone caught in it.

The beast leaped into the air again, landing behind the throng of living and dead, swiping at a several of the shovel-wielding townsfolk with its tail. It took off, running headlong into Wesson's shop, smashing it to bits. The great reptile bounded about in the rubble like a sadistic puppy before setting sights on the apartments.

The dragon's jaws opened and it tried once more to spit fire. Wads of phlegm slammed into the walls. Trilgor rushed through the Watchmen and the towns- folk, grabbing a rifle from a stunned Watchman. Trilgor fired a wild shot at the beast, getting its atten- tion. The bullet bounced off the side of its head. Eyes of death turned towards Trilgor. They stared each other down for long moment. The beast blinked first with a bellowing roar. Trilgor replied in kind and shouldered the rifle, firing as it charged him. The dragon's left eye exploded, making it veer off on instinct. When its head snapped back towards Trilgor, it glared at him with a new intensity while its left eye knit back together.

"Now I've really stepped in it," Trilgor whispered

to himself.

The dragon snarled at him and then opened its mouth to let loose another roar. Nothing came out. The beast seized and began dry-heaving. Its shoulders working to steady itself, its head bobbing up and down with each convulsion. With its jaw lowered and throat convulsing, Trilgor could see more of the phlegm working its way out of its throat. And flame.

"Gods damn," he muttered.

One last gasping wretch and the huge wad exited its host violently, slamming into the ground, splattering everywhere. Not even a moment behind it came fiery coughs. Flames licked its mouth. The dragon stood in its full glory once more. It growled in what Trilgor could've only described as a sadistic laugh.

Flames spewed forth from the beast's maw. Trilgor lifted the rifle, aiming at its eyes again but it turned away and lit up the pile of wood that had once been Wesson's shop, the whole thing going up immediately, turning into a great bonfire. The dragon spun, spitting flames all around itself. The flames licked the apartments, catching curtains in broken windows. Jhaan's shop caught fire as well, lighting from the inferno that was now Wesson's shop. Trilgor gulped and knew in his heart that Greenreach Bluffs was going to burn to the ground.

****

Selbie's heart wanted to crash through his rib cage and disappear, beating with despair and fury and horror. His sweat was like liquid fear. He held on to Sadie's shoulder tightly, the revolver's barrel pressed hard and trembling against Sadie's skull. He jerked as the hunter came bounding up the stairs but as soon as Grimluk got to the top, he gave his command.

Sadie looked at Grimluk, trying to remain strong. When her boss had come running back home, he'd surprised her, taking her hostage and making her help him retrieve Ald'n's corpse from the cellar. She was scared but stood defiantly.

"I don't know how you managed to beat them but you take one step closer and I'll splatter her brains everywhere before I do the same to yours," Selbie said with a hiss.

Grimluk held up his hands, trying for diplomacy. "You need to call them off. You heard that roar. There's a fucking dragon out there and it's destroying your town."

"Fuck the town! And fuck orcs! I let that pissant and her son into the town and how does she repay me? She kills the vampire I hired to make me immortal. Then you show up and between you and Trilgor, I think I've had all I can stand of orcs. All you do is get in the way." Selbie's eyes were bloodshot and beyond wild. He was drunk on fear and anger.

"You did all this to gain *immortality*?" Grimluk replied.

"Why should I have to die?! There are so many ways to live on but you hunters, all of you, just take them from us. What right do you have?!"

Grimluk's jaw set, realizing there was no chance at all to get through to the man.

"Why don't you just get down on your fucking knees and put a bullet in your head for me, hm?" Selbie suggested, beads of sweat pouring down his face.

"You die, the demon makes me immortal, everyone wins. Go on!"

Grimluk very slowly opened his coat, revealing his revolver. He looked from the old man to Sadie. She shook her head.

"Do it!" Selbie screamed. "Do it now!"

Grimluk looked at Sadie again while Selbie goaded him, his hand inching towards the butt of his pistol.

"Don't!" Sadie cried. She grunted as Selbie drilled the barrel into her skull. Something in her mind came undone then and she decided to do something completely reckless. As the mayor started to speak again, she slammed her elbow straight into his balls. The sheer surprise of the blow froze him entirely and she spun away from his grip. The ridiculous, stupid luck of his reaction made her shiver for years after.

Grimluk drew like lightning. The gun barked and Selbie's pistol exploded, shredding his hand with shrapnel and shattering his fingers. Grimluk pistol-whipped him before he could begin to scream, knocking him back onto the big desktop. He rushed forward and ripped the amulet off Selbie's neck.

"STOP!" Grimluk yelled, clutching the thing tightly. It flashed, bathing his hand in pale light.

CHAPTER 13

Gwen ran out of the temple, the only thought in her mind to get to her father. She passed through the center of town as the dragon prepared to leap in and begin its bout of destruction. She neared the crowd and screamed, "Daddy!" hoping he'd hear her. Tears rolled down her cheeks as Trilgor rushed past her, following the dragon's leap, his focus entirely on the beast.

Gwen screamed again and this time, Peter heard his daughter's call. The Watchman barreled through groups of fighting people, swinging his rifle like a club as he yelled his child's name. Peter ran as hard as he could when he saw Gwen standing behind everyone, watching in horror as Trilgor started a fight with a dragon. He scooped Gwen up and ran for the Watch, stopping just outside.

"Gwenny, what are you doing?! Where's Momma? Where's your brother?" Peter asked frantically, tumbling over the words. Gwen's mouth screwed up.

"B-brother k..." she took a deep breath. "Brother k-killed Momma!" The sobs exploded.

"What? No, no, honey, Nicholas is a good boy, no, what happ-" Peter's head spun around at the

191

sound of falling bodies. The dead had pushed the Watchmen and townsfolk away and were running towards Selbie's house with abandon. Some of them ended up pinned down with the disgusting black phlegm the dragon had been spitting, but most were rapidly approaching the backside of Greenreach Bluffs.

The Watchmen and townsfolk alike had tried desperately to hold back the wrath of the dead while avoiding the dragon's reach. Peter watched as Trilgor kept the dragon's focus on him, firing his rifle dry.

"Gwenny, run instead and hide. Don't come out until I come get you, okay?" Peter kissed his daughter's head. She nodded, wiping away tears and disappeared into the Watch. "Gods damn it," Peter cursed to himself as he took off to help his captain.

As the horde of dead got into Selbie's tiny courtyard, a pale flash of light filled the town. They all skidded to a halt, Selbie's will now replaced by Grimluk's command. They all stood still as stone, waiting to be released or ordered. The dragon, however, paused just long enough to register that it had been told to stop. It looked back towards Selbie's house and seemed to scoff, seemed to say, "I'm too powerful for you," before turning back to Trilgor, who had been joined by the other Watchman. Peter lifted his rifle and fired and like his captain, he shot the scaly terror in the eye. This time, the dragon's right eye took the bullet.

The beast glared at them both, every fiber of its being filling with malice, and stalked closer. Peter fired again and again, emptying the rifle's tube, each shot finding an eye or bouncing off a horn. Out of ammo, Trilgor shouted, "Come and get me, you dumb piece of troll shit!"

Fire welled up in the beast's throat. Flames exploded out with vicious force. Peter pushed Trilgor as hard as he could, sending his captain sliding away in a cloud of dust. The dragon's breath engulfed the man. He tried to scream but flames shot down his throat, scorching his insides.

The fire died away and the air around Peter shimmered with residual heat. Every inch of him was charred and smoking. His hair all burned away, portions of skin melting off, eyes now black pieces of shrunken charcoal. Peter's body collapsed with a dull thud, a cloud of dust puffing up around him.

Trilgor had no chance to process what had happened. The unexpected shove had caused him to hit his head, dazing him. Before he could even think about standing, the dragon crushed his right leg, breaking every bone in it with a loud, wet crunch. Trilgor howled in pain as the beast pinned him to the ground, its heavy claw on his chest, puffing hot air in his face from its nostrils. Trilgor squirmed, trying to get free but it was no use. The dragon growled in pleasure.

Trilgor looked away as it blew the ghost of a flame in his face. Through squinting, watery eyes, he saw the glimmer of his rifle. Desperate fingers reached for the gun, as the beast watched. It reached over with its tail and flicked the gun into Trilgor's hand. He looked up into its obsidian face. The dragon's mouth peeled back into a toothy approximation of a smile.

"Yeah, fuck you too," Trilgor said before swinging the rifle at the creature's eye.

The dragon's head wobbled to the side, the strength of the blow surprising it for a moment. It snapped back to its prey, who swung again. Its jaws opened in an instant, biting down on the weapon and shattered it. Fire roiled in its throat as it prepared to burn and shred Trilgor in triumph. It breathed in, mouth open in a fierce display of flames.

Trilgor gave a violent start as a hole exploded in the side of the dragon's neck, the sound of a gunshot echoing out. The flames died instantly but the beast's hold on him remained. It looked around for the source of the shot. There was Grimluk, revolver in hand, aiming at the beast's maw. It tried to roar but couldn't. It tried to burn him in its mighty fire but only coughed up black blood instead.

The ancient terror felt a command in its mind. The amulet lit up again, shining its eldritch, purple light from between Grimluk's fingers. The dragon stepped away from Trilgor, who did his best to squirm away. Charlie ran up, grabbing his arms and dragging him off as quickly as she could. He gave a breathless thanks.

"Shut up, Cap'n," was all she said.

Grimluk watched as Charlie dragged Trilgor away from the dragon, its attention fully on him now as their wills battled. He walked towards it, holstering his revolver. Every ounce of his mind commanded it to return to death. The creature was ancient, powerful, and it would not go without a fight. Grimluk felt the dragon's will push back at him.

Behind him, a bleeding Selbie lay groaning, holding his hand, his jaw swollen and purple, but miraculously unbroken. Sadie stood over him. She looked up at Grimluk for a moment, watching the battle of wills unfold.

Grimluk felt blood trickle from his nose but he pushed on with a grunt. The dragon's head began to lull, a raspy growl sliding from its throat. He closed his eyes and pushed, his heart thundering in his chest. The dragon collapsed, reaching out sluggishly towards him, its talons spread wide. The hole in its neck started burning away as the skin began to decay rapidly. Its strength rapidly ebbing, the outstretched talons hitting the ground limply. It gnashed its teeth and whipped out its mighty tail in spite, enough strength left to put a hole in the Silver Sliver. With one, final pull of its fading life force, it gave one last vain effort to spit fire at Grimluk. The last threads of life fell away along with the dragon's flesh and muscle, its body once more nothing but the skeleton that had been buried under a thousand years of erosion. Grimluk collapsed to his knees, out of breath and dizzy. The amulet fell from his hand into the dirt. The horde of dead all collapsed where they were, returning to eternal slumber once more.

"Is it over?" Sadie asked.

"Yeah," Grimluk said with a grimace, "yeah, it's over." Little cuts dotted his face, and a big bruise was forming on his cheek as he wiped the blood from his nose away on the back of his hand. He scooped the amulet back up, shoving it and bits of dirt into his pocket. He got to his feet slowly, waiting for the dizziness to pass. Grimluk bent down, clamping a hand over Selbie's ankle and started dragging the old man, around the dragon's bones, towards Trilgor and the other survivors. "Trilgor," Grimluk called.

"Grimluk," the captain responded. "You did it."

"Yeah. And I brought you a present." Grimluk all

but slung Selbie at the Watchmen. "This colossal ass-hole is why your mother's dead."

"What?!" Trilgor roared, sitting up.

"This all happened because he wanted immortality. He somehow hired that vampire to come and turn him and the gods damned demon promised him the same." Grimluk looked around at the crowd. They were muttering and talking to themselves. He saw where it was going and spoke to them. "I can see what you're thinking, folks, and lynching this fucker isn't gonna make you feel better and it's definitely not gonna fix things. I know you probably don't believe me but that's a road you don't want to go down, even if this...pustule deserves it. There's been enough death today."

The people looked at him silently for a long time, trying to make up their minds on the matter. A few thought about arguing with Grimluk but the image of him putting a dragon down played in their minds. The excitement was wearing off too and they began to sober up from it. Most of them sullenly agreed and just collapsed into the dirt where they stood. They could decide what to do with Selbie later. Even if they decided to rip him apart.

"Where's Ivor?" Grimluk asked Trilgor.

"Don't know. Reckon he's in the temple trying to figure out why the barrier went down. Haven't seen him since he took off after it fell. Sure would be nice if he'd bring me something for my leg though."

"Fuck your leg, what about my hand?" Selbie mumbled. Sadie laughed at the sound of his voice through the swollen jaw.

"Selbie, you're lucky to be alive right now, quit

your bellyachin',” Trilgor replied. “You're lucky I don't shoot you myself.”

Sadie thought for a moment about giving the old man a stiff kick but decided against it. “Don't forget about your balls, old man,” she said instead. “How are those?”

Selbie groaned. Trilgor looked at Sadie, a huge grin spread across his face. “I guess someone should patch the bastard up and stick him in a cell.”

“I'll do it,” Grimluk said, picking Selbie up off the ground. “Glad to return the favor.” He marched Selbie into the Watch and planted him in a chair. He set to work bandaging the old man's hand quickly and tightly, not bothering to splint the fingers, before shoving Selbie into the same cell he'd stood in earlier that morning. “Enjoy your new living space, old man. Sadie won't be serving you dinner anymore.”

“What happened?” Negos asked from the other end of the room.

“It's over, Negos,” Grimluk replied.

“You killed the demon?!”

“Mm...not exactly. Been a bit busy but I'll be finishing that shortly. Trilgor will fill you in later.” As Grimluk left, Negos just nodded silently. A moment later, Gwen rushed out from her hiding spot and latched on to him. “What are you doing here, little one?”

“Daddy said not to come out before he got me but I got scared and I saw you putting Mr. Mayor in jail,” she said, looking up at him.

“It's safe now, let's go find your dad.” Grimluk took Gwen's hand in his and led her outside. They looked around for a moment before asking Trilgor where Peter was.

Trilgor sighed, rubbing the bridge of his nose. He looked at Gwen with a heavy heart. "Dead. I'm sorry, kiddo. He pushed me out of the way of the dragon's fire. Your father died a hero."

Gwen's bottom lip began to quiver as tears welled up in her eyes. Her body jolted and then the Spirit spoke. "Orc, I can spare the child for a moment. She has suffered greatly this day. You hold the means to lessen that suffering."

Grimluk pulled the amulet from his coat pocket. The dust he'd gathered with it slid off cleanly, leaving it bare. He stared at it for a long moment, those nearby watching Gwen in confusion and fear. Grimluk looked at the amulet and called out, "Peter." It flashed.

Peter's corpse sucked in a deep, choking breath. His eyes opened up to a blinding, clear sky, the sunlight filling the air with a dry heat that threatened to take away any moisture it shone on. His charred skin began to heal itself, the black flecks falling away as it returned to its former, healthy tan. He stood, slowly, looking around. He saw the dragon's bones and remembered, he'd died. He saw the crowd of survivors, Gwen standing next to Grimluk, and started jogging over. He stopped as he got close, looking up at Grimluk.

"Why are her eyes black, Grimluk? What happened?" Peter asked hoarsely.

"First, put this on," Grimluk said, setting down his bag before handing Peter his coat. The man's body had been restored for the moment, but his clothes were still black ash. Peter slipped the coat on, buttoning it closed. For a moment, he looked like a boy in his father's coat.

Gwen's body trembled. She looked up at her father and squealed through tears, "Daddy!" She raced over, wrapping her arms around his leg. "Daddy, why are you wearing Mr. Grimluk's coat?"

Peter picked his daughter up and hugged her for a long time. She squeezed his neck and gave him a kiss on the cheek. Finally, he sat her back down, kneeling with her. "Gwenny, where's your Momma and brother?"

The tears welled up again, Gwen's eyes red and puffy now. "I told you, brother killed-" her breath caught in her throat, causing a lone sob. Finally, she just took her father's hand and began to lead him to the temple. Grimluk followed behind them. The trio walked in silence, tears streaming down Gwen's face. Gwen stopped a little ways inside and then just pointed. Peter walked over and gasped.

"Cassie!" he shouted, rushing over to his wife's half-buried corpse. One of her hands sat above the stone and he grabbed it. It was cold. "No no no no, no, baby, please," he said, shaking her hand.

Ivor had wandered out at the sound of the shout. He walked quietly over to Peter, Grimluk meeting him. "I'm sorry," Ivor said. "I found her here. I made the rock soft so I wouldn't have to fight her."

Peter wheeled on the old magician. "Get her the fuck out of there, old man!"

Ivor planted his staff next to her again, beginning his chant as he had previously, his voice flowing out in a soft melody. Grimluk called Cassie's name as the stone floor wavered and softened once more. He and Peter pulled her out as she came to, Ivor's chant dying away.

"What's going on?" Cassie asked in a daze. All Peter could do was embrace his wife. It surprised her but she smiled and hugged him back.

"Come here, little one," Grimluk called to Gwen. She hesitated but then walked over to her parents. The Quinns looked at their daughter and Peter remembered what Gwen had told him before he'd made her hide.

"Cass...Gwen...she said Nicholas killed you."

Cassie couldn't answer. She just started crying and nodded her head before burying her face into Peter's shoulder. Gwen hugged their legs very gently. Cassie reached down to pet her daughter's head, pulling back from Peter. They stood there for a long time. Ivor and Grimluk remained quiet.

"What happened?" Peter finally asked.

Cassie recounted what had happened, absently playing with Gwen's hair. Peter's jaw hung open in shock when she finished. "Why are you in that big coat?" she asked in return. He told her, and Gwen, what had happened.

Ivor looked over at Grimluk, finally noticing the amulet. Grimluk held up his other hand. The old magician frowned but nodded. They looked back at the Quinns in confusion as Peter started laughing. Cassie began to laugh as well, Gwen following shortly after her, giggling more at her parents than anything she found funny.

"Well how much worse could it get, huh? We're dead, our kids are possessed, our daughter's an orphan. The day's still young, right?" Peter said through fits of laughter at the absurdity of it all. He sighed, a few choked laughs slipping out. "We gotta find someone to take care of Gwen now..."

Cassie frowned, bending down to pick her daughter up. She kissed Gwen's head, looking at her husband. "At least," she started, "at least we can do that."

"I'll take her," Grimluk said, holding his hat to his chest. The Quinns looked at him. Peter's mouth opened, but he didn't know what to say. "The crowd saw the Spirit speak through her. For all they know it's a demon. Maybe I can find a way to get the thing out of her, maybe not, but I can keep her safe and teach her how to take care of herself." Grimluk smiled at Gwen. "And how to make her teeth strong." She smiled a toothy grin back.

Peter and Cassie looked at each other. Cassie closed her eyes, resting her face against Gwen's head and nodded. Peter looked back at Grimluk. "I...we...thank you."

"We'll let you say your goodbyes," Grimluk said, turning and walking outside. Ivor followed him. "If you've got a spot you prepare the dead, take the Quinns to it before I..." He let the words hang in the air.

"Yeah," Ivor replied distantly, watching the smoke from Jhaan and Wesson's shops billow, thick and black. Townsfolk worked to put the fires out, forming a bucket brigade but it didn't matter. The apartments had caught now and thick smoke was roiling out of the windows.

"You gonna be able to get the barrier back up?"

"I'll need to find another crystal first. Watchmen'll have to be extra vigilant until I get it back up. Or maybe we'll all just pack up and get the fuck out now."

Peter, Cassie, and Gwen stood where they were, huddled together in one last embrace. Peter and Cassie kissing their daughter's head and each other. Gwen struggling not to cry, understanding with clarity that this was the last time she would see her parents. Each of them whispered "I love you" over and over again. After a while, Cassie sat Gwen down. The Quinns took their daughter's hands and walked her outside, back into the glaring sunlight of the afternoon. Grimluk and Ivor turned as they approached.

"We're ready," Cassie said. She knelt down and hugged Gwen tightly. "Listen to Mr. Grimluk, sweetie. Be good. Stay safe. I love you."

Peter bent down to his daughter and kissed her head. "I love you, Gwen."

"I love you too, Momma. I love you too, daddy. I'll miss you." Gwen's lip quivered.

"I should give this back to you," Peter said to Grimluk, pulling off the hunter's big, black coat. Grimluk took it back, sliding his bag to the ground and slipped the coat back on. "You take good care of her or I'll find some way to come back and kick your ass."

"On my life. Ivor, I'll put the amulet away shortly." He held his hand out for Gwen's. She gave her parents one last kiss each and then took Grimluk's hand. He led her back towards the Watch. After a little while had past, he slipped the amulet into his bag. Peter and Cassie Quinn slipped back into death, holding each other's hands on the stone slab Ivor used to prepare the dead.

"I'm afraid I have some bad news," Grimluk told Trilgor a little while later.

"Well allow me to preface it with a hardy fuck you," the Watch captain responded dryly. Charlie was bent over, setting his crushed leg in a splint. He hissed in pain. "Easy!" Charlie rolled her eyes.

"It seems Gwen's brother made himself Priskus's new anchor by way of his mother. The Quinns are both dead."

"Ah, fuck," Trilgor said with a sigh. "What does that mean for us?"

"Priskus won't want to stick around. If the boy hasn't fled already, he will by tomorrow morning. That means, ultimately, that the town is demon-free but..."

"But?"

"I wouldn't call it a success," Grimluk finished. His upper lip rose in a half-sneer born of frustration.

Trilgor snorted. "I reckon not but at least we're free of it. Long as Ivor can get the barrier back up, we can rebuild too."

"He said it would take some time. You got enough of the Watch left to handle it?" Grimluk looked up at the crowd of survivors, Watchmen and miners mostly. The farmers had wandered away, back to their animals and meager crops, eager to forget the day's events.

"Until the barrier's back up, everyone's gonna have to work Watch duty," Trilgor replied. "And yes,

Charlie, I know I said I'd give you a month off-" She held up a hand, hushing him.

"I'll call it in later," she said and finished tying the splint off.

"I think we might want to consider just leaving the town," Sadie offered. "Sure, there's plenty left in the mine but is it worth it at this point?"

Orn spoke up. "You got a point there, Sadie. I'm sure we could all find work elsewhere. Guess we'll all have to figure that out." He dropped down next to Trilgor, scratching at his beard, splitting a gob of dried blood that had trickled down from around his eye. He'd been hit hard and it had swollen up as big as his fist.

The group looked towards the sudden sound of shouting. It was a wordless expression of excitement. A moment later, Edgar, the old halfling from the Sliver, came running out yipping and hollering. "I won!" he shouted over and over again. "By the gods, I finally won a fuckin' hand!" He didn't seem to register what had happened and disappeared toward the farm.

As everyone settled, some of the survivors who'd been listening and commenting among themselves came to a decision. One of them, a tiny elf woman with black hair and eyes the color of dusk, stepped forward. "Captain Trilgor, sir," she said.

"Yes?" He looked up at her from the ground.

"We've been thinkin' it over and given the facts, we'd uh..." she turned back towards the others, who looked away. Trilgor cleared his throat. "We'd feel safer if the hunter and the girl left. Things weren't as bad before he got here and she's got something evil in her."

After Trilgor picked his jaw back up, he started to respond but Grimluk spoke first. "We'll leave after I've filled my waterskins. I suspected after you saw what happened with Gwen that you'd feel that way. I promised the Quinns I'd take her with me and look after her." The woman looked away, shuffling her feet. The group mumbled apologies and dispersed, some of them joining the Watchmen in tending to the wounded, all of them ashamed.

"Well, I think ya done right by us, Grimluk," Orn said.

"There was no way you could've known all that was gonna happen," Charlie followed. "No fuckin' way anyone could of known."

"Fuck 'em," Sadie said, looking away.

"It's alright," Grimluk said with a sigh. "They're still scared. Maybe I can find something back at Hunter's Hollow and summon the bastard to seal it for good. At the least, maybe I can pull the Spirit out of Gwen." He looked down at the child.

"Help me up," Trilgor said to Charlie. After getting to his feet, he extended a hand to Grimluk. "Thanks for trying at least." Grimluk took Trilgor's hand.

"You ever decide to leave, any of you," Grimluk said, looking at the other three as well, "head northeast to Eagle's Point. It's a decent town not far from Hunter's Hollow. Send me a message by magi-tell, I'll get it and find ya." He shook Charlie, Orn, and Sadie's hands in turn. "Tell Ivor thanks for all his help."

"I will," Trilgor said with a nod.

Grimluk reached down, opening his hand for Gwen. She reached up and took it. "Come, little one."

Grimluk led Gwen away, stopping at the well to refill their waterskins. A small crowd reformed, watching as the giant hunter and his tiny new charge walked away, heading out into the Wastelands.

"I'm sorry for all of this, little one," Grimluk said after silent hours of walking.

"I told you, Orc, you brought salvation," the Spirit replied instead of Gwen.

"You knew."

"Yes."

"And you just let it happen."

"I did what I could. Being bound to this child inhibits me," the Spirit said with a sigh.

Grimluk remained quiet for a time. "When we get to Border Rest, the three of us need to have a talk about your place in the world."

"Very well," it said, receding once more.

"I heard it that time, Mr. Grimluk," Gwen said a moment later. "I want it to be quiet for now." They continued on in silence with the sun beating down on their backs, their shadows growing longer as the sun sank behind them.

Late that night, long after Grimluk and Gwen had made it to Border Rest, Kenton Selbie sat alone in his cell, sleeping on the canvas cot that now served as his bed. He jerked awake as a blizzard chill ran down his spine. Nicholas stared into his face, squatting down in front of him. The boy's eyes reflected the meager light like a wolf's. Terror welled up in Selbie in unfathomable waves as the boy smiled at him with a wolf's smile. Nicholas took something from his belt and held it out to the old man as he sat up. Selbie stared down at the crude knife that had cut him the night before.

"No, please, I did what you asked," he whispered to the demon-boy.

"And you failed. You know what to do."

The next morning, when Charlie came to bring Selbie breakfast, she cried out. The corpse of Kenton Selbie lay upright, slack jawed, with two long gashes down each wrist and a puddle of dried blood under him, brown and thick. No one could figure out how he did it. No one mourned him.

Grimluk and Gwen spent days holed up in a room at Border Rest. The morning after their arrival, he had first informed the bounty board officer that the job in Greenreach Bluffs was done. After that, he took Gwen out to get new clothes, boots, and a hat. While they waited on the boots and clothes to be made, he sat Gwen down in their room at the Dancing Dwarf.

"Little one, there's a lot I'm gonna have to teach you. We have a long way to go. But first, we need to set some ground rules for the Spirit. I'm sure it can hear me."

"Yeah," Gwen said.

"We'll figure out if we can pull it out eventually. In the meantime, it needs to work with you, from inside. No more coming out. No more black eyes."

"It says okay, Mr. Grimluk."

"Good. We have a long journey ahead of us and even more to show you," Grimluk said. "The best place to start is with your boots."

"My boots?"

"Yes. A tiny bit of blood magic. Folks fear blood magic but when done right, it can create lasting effects. It will hurt, but some of your blood can be used to enchant your boots so that you'll never get lost. It's how I made it through the dust storm when I arrived."

When her things were ready, Grimluk prepared to walk her through the ritual. Gwen made him promise to give her a hug whenever she asked before she would do it. There was no flash of light, no energy, just a sense of sureness that filled her feet after she put the boots on.

"You're my family now, Gwen. My sister," Grimluk said as they left Border Rest shortly after. Gwen squeezed his hand but said nothing.

RECOMMENDED AUTHORS

You've read my book now (and thank you for that!), and I'd imagine you'll be hungry for something new so here are a few recommendations for folks I know and enjoyed.

James Jakins, Author of *Jack Bloodfist: Fixer*.
Rachel Sharp, Author of the *Planetary Tarantella* and *Phaethon* series.
M.Todd Gallowglas, Storyteller & Author of the *Dead Weight*, *Tears of Rage*, & *Halloween Jack* series.
Amalia Dillin, Author of the *Orcs Saga*
Edward M. Erdelac, Author of the *Merkabah Rider* series.
Krista D. Ball, Author of the *Tales of Tranquility* and *Spirit Caller* series.

Happy reading, everyone!

ABOUT THE AUTHOR

Ashe grew up watching and reading about adventures and having horrible nightmares. He spent most of his young life wanting to know more about what scared him but also doing so from between fingers and from under the covers. Eventually, the realm of nightmares became home. Heroes and villains and the struggle of Good against Evil, combined with Horror, helped mold him into the weirdo lover–of–the–strange that he is. Ashe lives in Tulsa, OK with his partner.

Where you can find Ashe on the web

ashearmstrong.com
patreon.com/ashearmstrong
twitter.com/ashearmstrong
facebook.com/ashearmstrong
goodreads.com/ashearmstrong

www.ingramcontent.com/pod-product-compliance
Lightning Source LLC
Chambersburg PA
CBHW021138130626
46554CB00005B/1563